THE McCALLUM BOYS

Most folks either love or hate the McCallum boys. Everyone fears them. Their father brought them up to Wyoming from Texas and died, leaving them half-grown and rough-tempered. To their neighbours on the Porter ranch, Rose Ann and her niece Becky, the McCallum boys are helpful, attentive and polite. When Rose Ann hires a man from Medicine Bow to drive her horse herd to market, she discovers he has more on his mind for her and Becky than a few chores — but he has not yet met the McCallum boys . . .

Books by C. J. Sommers
in the Linford Western Library:

GHOST RANCH
COMES A HORSEMAN
THE OUTLAW'S DAUGHTER
THE LONESOME DEATH
OF JOE SAVAGE
CLIMAX
SKELETON HAND
WHITE WIND
LONGSHOT
THE SHOESTRINGERS
PIRATES OF THE DESERT

C. J. SOMMERS

THE McCALLUM BOYS

Complete and Unabridged

LINFORD
Leicester

First published in Great Britain in 2016 by
Robert Hale
an imprint of The Crowood Press
Wiltshire

First Linford Edition
published 2019
by arrangement with
The Crowood Press
Wiltshire

A catalogue record for this book is available
from the British Library.

ISBN 978–1–4448–4211–1

Published by
F. A. Thorpe (Publishing)
Anstey, Leicestershire

Set by Words & Graphics Ltd.
Anstey, Leicestershire
Printed and bound in Great Britain by
T. J. International Ltd., Padstow, Cornwall

This book is printed on acid-free paper

1

It was a clear, bright, and cool morning in the Wyoming plains. The trees in the forested country stood in deep, proud ranks. Out on the open terrain the grass stood mostly long but yellowed to an autumn color. Mounds of gray boulders, assembled in a random arrangement by nature, dotted the land, rising to head height on a mounted man as the meadow proceeded west towards the far off Rocky Mountains, and the hummocks and rock stacks became more numerous.

Here and there were clusters of oak trees having a tough time of it this time of year. Farther on yet lay a deep-cut coulee where willow trees and an occasional cottonwood survived along its banks.

The coulee was a thirty-foot scar across the dry grassland. Sheer sides and sandy bottom, it had to be crossed to reach

the stronghold stone house of the no-
torious McCallum boys.

★   ★   ★

The McCallum boys had their own special way in and back out of the coulee.
The route could not be discerned easily.
It had even once escaped detection by
an army scout. The coulee was a natural
fortification as daunting as any moat,
and of course the house itself, built of
gray Wyoming granite, was nearly impregnable. Of the four boys you could bet
that at least one of them would be on
guard. If they were out on one of their
escapades, you would find one stationed
with his rifle at the house's narrow windows or behind the walls of the stone-
walled corral.

That corral had been one of their
father's proudest achievements. Down
in Nacogdoches he had seen a man
shot dead by a bullet between the rail
posts of a more usual corral, and it had
affected him enough to conclude that

wooden corrals were natural death traps.

The four-foot high walls of the McCallum corral could not be penetrated by anything so simple as a lead bullet. He used to brag about that wall and the house as he got older over a dram of whiskey. And he drank more whiskey than ever because of the pain left behind by adventures of his own. These agonies, he had concluded, were saved until a man has reached the end of his days to deliver their full brunt.

'They're by introduction of what's come,' he told his sons, 'sometimes hurtful enough to make you yearn for mere frying.'

The old man would be seated in front of the fire in the ox-sized fireplace in his very large and quite sturdy rocking chair, alternately reminiscing and expounding his rather odd philosophy. The boys had soaked it all up.

Josiah McCallum, still known as 'Steamboat Bill' by those who knew of his rough days in Texas, had been a man of wide reputation in earlier days.

It was said that his name had been printed more times on posters than Shakespeare's. Maybe — here in the Far West there weren't many men who even knew the name Bill Shakespeare, but there were almost none who had not heard of Steamboat Bill McCallum.

Old Bill knew of another ex-river pilot named Dick King. He'd had done well for himself by giving up the river and taking up the land. Richard King now had himself a nice little spread down near Corpus Christi of over 800,000 acres. He had more cattle than a hound has fleas, and so much money that only God could count it. Yeah, the old boy had done all right for himself.

It was with that in mind that Bill McCallum had driven a small herd of mixed-breed cattle and a dozen horses out of Texas to the far north, searching for open land that he could similarly profit on. Three other men, tired of the life on the river, had come along. After their first winter in Wyoming all three men had returned to Texas on a flatboat.

Bill had a small wagon, which his wife, Carolyn, had to drive much of the way with her baby at her side. This was McCallum's first son christened Rodeo (pronounced in the Mexican way as Ro-day-oh with a hard accent on the second syllable), for no reason anyone ever understood. McCallum told anyone who inquired that he had had his fill of Jims, Bills and Johns. He continued this line of thinking with his next three sons, the last of which cost the life of Carolyn McCallum with his birthing.

She had lived to see Wyoming and the long stretch of open land Bill McCallum claimed as his own, but not much longer, and she was held up by Bill as a saint to the four boys: Rodeo, Nicodemus, Wyndom and Kittery. The boys inevitably acquired nicknames — except for Rodeo, who refused to be called Rod — and were known far and wide across the territory as Nick, Wynn, and Kit — the McCallum boys. They grew up to be good friends to have, bad enemies to acquire, skunks, gun-happy killers or Samaritans depending on who you talked to and what day of the week it was.

It was said they came by it naturally — what else could you expect the sons of Bill McCallum to be? Old Bill was a man who took care of business in his way, and that way frequently included the use of guns — and never left a debt unpaid.

This last was underscored on his death-bed. Charlie Bent and Walt Dims — two neighboring ranchers who had never gotten along with Steamboat Bill — decided that it was only the Christian thing to do to go by McCallum's house and say goodbye to Bill as he was not long for it.

They found Bill propped up in bed, his old gray head sagging on his chest, his face unshaven, his eyes watering. Charlie Bent went up to the bedside first and told Bill that he was sorry they had not gotten along better, and that he would try to help Bill's sons if they needed it. Bill nodded his head and waved his hand as Charlie stepped away.

When it was Walt Dims' turn he took his hat in his hand and came forward. Before he had spoken a word, Bill said, 'You think I've forgotten those four prime steers you rustled from me?'

Then the .44 Colt which Bill had hidden beneath his blankets spoke and punched a smoldering hole right through Walt Dims' shirt over his heart. With that debt paid, Bill dropped his heavy revolver on the floor and closed his eyes. He would never open them again. Walt staggered back and fell dead on the bedroom floor. Charlie Bent made a rapid exit from the McCallum house.

'Well, he always was a hard one,' was all Marshal Bleeker had to say when Charlie Bent reported the murder. 'Beside, you tell me McCallum is dead, so what can I do? We quit hanging dead men some time ago.'

'You'd best start keeping a close eye on those McCallum boys, Marshal,' Charlie Bent responded. 'Without the old man to keep a tight rein on them, there's no telling what they'll get up to.'

The McCallum boys seemed bound to make a prophet of Charlie Bent.

Harry Stout was destined to become one of the first victims of the McCallum boys once they became free of all restraints with the passing of old Bill. If Steamboat Bill could have foreseen what he had loosed on the world . . . but then again, perhaps he wouldn't have cared, being very much inclined that way himself.

But Harry Stout had no idea what sort of young men the McCallum boys were, and he paid a price for his ignorance.

It was Rodeo, the oldest of the McCallum boys, with whom Harry Stout had that little mix-up, over at the Eagle Eye Saloon in Collier, which served as the county seat. Stout just didn't seem to be able to understand Rodeo's way of thinking about matters.

The two men and several companions had been playing poker and drinking raw whiskey for three hours that evening, and Stout was feeling pretty good about the result of the card game. He had a moderate sized stack of blue chips in front of him and two good-sized stacks of red. The white were strewn in a loose pile. In short, Harry Stout was winning big.

He was a round man with ginger hair and mustache, his face glowing with the flush of success. Stout leaned back in his chair and stretched his arms overhead. With a glance at his steel railroad watch which rested on the table next to his new-found riches, he announced.

'It's been fun, boys, but I guess it's about time for me to hit the streets.'

'You're quitting?' Rodeo McCallum asked, his eyes narrow and hard.

'I try to quit when I'm ahead,' Stout answered, still smiling.

There was a long pause while Stout scraped his poker chips together, forming neat stacks. Rodeo hadn't moved and the other two players, looking nervous, eased their chairs back from the table. It seemed that Harry Stout was unaware of the local rules of poker.

'I like to win,' Rodeo said in a low even voice. Harry Stout continued to smile.

'Why, sure. We all do.'

Rodeo's stare became hard and still. 'If I can't win,' he said in a soft murmur, 'I don't care to lose.' Stout looked up from the chips, his expression now blank as he tried to be amiable without understanding the situation. A third man at the table, Walter Gage, owner of the town's small grain mill, explained: 'Around here we return Rodeo's losings to him if he's had a run of bad luck. The rest of the winnings stay with the winner, of course.'

'That's absurd!' Stout said, shifting in his chair in a way which caused Rodeo to become wary. 'We can all lose, but this man . . . ' He gestured with an angry finger. 'This man has his losses returned. What makes him so special?'

'He don't like to lose,' Gage advised Stout. A single drop of perspiration had broken free of his forehead and now trickled into the miller's eyes. He wiped it away and backed from the table, looking around for help. Someone ought to be able to explain things better. Men just did not say no to Rodeo McCallum. They all had fun at the regular card games. Everyone won some, lost some. But Rodeo never lost — he would not allow it, and everyone let him have his way. What were they to do, tell him he could not sit in at their table? They never raked his coins in.

It beat getting your eyeballs shot out.

And Rodeo was good enough to do that with a .44.

'All right, boys,' Harry Stout said, rising from the table. 'You've had your fun with me.' Stout's smile had returned, but it was a wavering expression. 'You, mister,' he said to Rodeo, 'I don't care if you're Father Christmas or the devil. You sat down to our table and you have to take the same chances as everyone else.'

Then Harry Stout made his big mistake. He pulled out his pocket pistol to emphasize his point as he eased away from the table. It was not enough gun and he was not enough man. Rodeo McCallum shot him from under the table with his big Colt .44. Stout's arms flung skyward, the little pistol clattered onto the table as he screamed in agony. The .44 slug had taken him in the thigh bone, shattering it, and he dropped immediately to the floor of the saloon where he writhed, cursing and praying and shouting all at once. Not a man moved to aid him though the floor was heavy with spilled blood. Rodeo McCallum stood over Stout still, his revolver dangling from his hand.

'Since you're a stranger here,' Rodeo said, 'I'll leave you with one good leg.' Stout, still cursing and moaning didn't realize that Rodeo seriously thought that he was doing the man a favor.

* * *

It was still early in the day, just having passed noon, when Wynn McCallum wheeled the wagon drawn by two neat black horses into yard of the Porter house, a small, square, white-painted building sitting alone on the prairie. Four newly planted honey locust trees standing in a row cast only meager shade; farther on was a one gnarled black oak tree, which from its breadth seemed to have been planted sometime before the first Indian had yet arrived. Its trunk was twisted and lumpy; only a handful of slender green shoots sprouted out of it, giving hope each spring that these would grow into limbs as the year progressed. They never did; the tree and the land were too stubborn.

Wynn McCallum had no more than set his brake than the matronly figure of the Duchess, Rose Ann Porter, that is, emerged from the tiny house and onto the narrow porch, dusting her hands on her apron. The scent of freshly baked apple pie arrived with her. She lifted her eyes and waved an arm in greeting.

'Step down, Wynn, and have a slice of pie — it should be cooled enough!'

'No thanks, Duchess. You'll have to save me some for another time. I just stopped because the horses were thirsty and my posterior was getting numb.'

'Well, you know where the trough is,' Rose Ann called back. She was a house woman by inclination, and the best example of that sort of woman: cheerful, well-padded, eager to cook for a man at any excuse. She tolerated no tough talk or rough ways in her house. When Wynn had spoken of his *posterior* being sore from the pounding of the wooden seat, it was the word Rose Ann had taught him to use in place of the more ordinary terms. Hearing it caused her smile to widen, the twinkle in her eyes to brighten. She liked this young man. She was fond of all of the McCallum brothers, perhaps Wynn the most. She would not stand to hear them bad-mouthed. Any job she needed done around the ranch would be willingly taken up by the McCallum boys.

Wynn adored the woman; all of the

boys did, even the flint-faced Rodeo. Each of the boys felt sure that their own mother must have been like the Duchess. None would do a thing to slight her. Wynn picked one of the honey locust pods from a tree to chew on as he led the horses to water and dropped their bits for them. He watched them drink for a minute then decided he had better go up to the house. The Duchess might have her feelings hurt if he did not at least stop in and say hello.

There was that sense of duty, and then there was —

Oh, but there she was! A delicate skull with a shiny cap of fine, platinum hair. Wynn took a shy step toward the girl, removing his hat. Becky Porter, for her part, took an even shyer step away. Becky, the niece of the Duchess, was an extraordinarily pretty, neat package. She was over five feet tall — just barely. Each time Wynn saw her, he felt a primitive urge to wrap his large ungainly arms around her and protect her. From what, he did not know — all of the troubles of the world, he supposed.

'There's pie,' said Becky, by way of welcome. Well, what had he expected? He knew that he was a big awkward lunk. Like his brothers he had a fair set of shoulders, dark eyes, and wide mouth, but his features were not set in an attractive way like Rodeo's or Kit's. Rodeo was flat-out handsome when he was not intent on being angry. Nick was also a good-looking man, but he had no interest in accenting it by doing things like brushing his hair, or even bathing and shaving. Kit was handsome, but in a boyish way. He had a good, open smile which the girls found attractive, but he was still unformed in Wynn's critical vision — still just a boy.

And what was Becky but a girl? The two were better matched for each other. Now and then Wynn found himself jealous of his younger brother. Certainly Becky and Kit found things to talk about that Wynn found distant from him or beneath his concern.

He sighed, smiled, and followed Becky into the Duchess's kitchen. Becky crossed the room and dutifully removed a plate and cup to serve Wynn his pie and a cup of coffee.

Aunt Rose Ann stopped her.

'Wynn said that he hasn't the time to stop and eat today, Becky.' The woman was no fool; she assessed Wynn's expression and then let her glance include Becky. 'Unless he's changed his mind now.'

Wynn hesitated, but he knew that Nick would be at home waiting and watching for him.

'I'd better be on my way,' he said with some regret. Becky looked vaguely relieved.

'As you wish,' the Duchess said. 'There are going to be a few changes around here that I wanted to mention to you. But if you're going right home, Kit can tell you about those. He and Becky spent quite a while chatting this morning.'

Wynn McCallum only nodded. His thoughts, if they could have been heard just then, would have been little more than an angry growl.

'I'd better be going,' he said. 'I'll ask Kit later. Is this something that all of us need to know about?'

'Yes, oh yes! I would say so — well, no use telling the same story twice,' the Duchess told him. 'Kit knows — you ask him.'

Before he left Aunt Rose Ann gave Wynn a box containing an apple pie. 'I only baked two pies this time. You boys take this one. I know that a single pie is little more than a snack for four strapping young men. For that I apologize, but I also know you McCallum boys are like most men — baking a pie for yourselves is something you'd never do.'

Wynn McCallum thanked the Duchess richly and started the two blacks on their way homeward, the pie beside him on the seat. He had only one final glimpse of Becky Porter before the trees in the yard screened her from his view. She seemed happy, relieved as Wynn pulled away. That unvoiced growl formed itself again deep in his throat. He snapped the reins against the blacks' haunches unnecessarily.

Wynn rolled the wagon on across the plains unhappily. He disliked using the wagon at any time. The concealed crossing that the McCallum boys used to cross the coulee was just not wide enough for such contraptions. At times only two wheels had purchase. Kit had nearly lost a horse there. The kid had saved the animal only by sliding down and cutting it free of its harnesses.

Nevertheless, Nick had sent Wynn on a job and he would see it through as best he could. Once on the far side of the coulee with a few tight scrapes behind him, he lined the wagon out toward the horse herd where Nick was supposed to meet his younger brother near the lone oak. Wynn did not know if Nick would be there waiting for him or not. Any meeting with Nick McCallum was more or less a game of chance. It was utterly unlike a date with Rodeo — when Rodeo said be there at noon, you had damned well better be there at noon. Nick would be there when he could — if he hadn't changed his mind in the meantime.

Wynn thought that Nick would be there today. The appointment was an important one.

Wynn held the black horses to an easy trot and the grasslands flowed past rapidly, smoothly. The big oak was visible in the distance now — old, shaggy, broad. It was not a gnarled, broken specimen like the one standing in the yard of the Duchess, but seemed to be of the same age — ancient. Wynn's father guessed that the oaks had been two of the corner markers of the original landholder's spread, whoever he had been. But neither Steamboat Bill nor any of his sons had ever gotten curious enough about this theory to go hunting for the other two oaks, though they must still exist somewhere, if only as stumps.

Wynn now saw the oak tree in definition, boughs thick and drooping, rough-barked trunk and lightning-struck crown showing the wear of a hundred years. Beneath the tree stood Nick's red roan with its distinctive three white stockings and blaze, and squatting on his heels beside the roan, Nick McCallum himself in his torn hat, face unshaven as always, watching Wynn's approach with narrowed dark eyes. Now Nick rose, waiting to welcome his brother.

He did, with 'Took you long enough!' for a greeting.

'It's a little way from Rambler Shack,' Wynn answered without warmth. It didn't bother Nick McCallum a bit. He was immune to insult and regarded other people's feelings as mere chaff falling around his perfectly centered world. In short, Nick McCallum could not be insulted or held responsible for his actions by other people.

Nick McCallum did as he pleased whenever it pleased him without a shadow of guilt ever disturbing him. Other people only faintly existed in his life.

'You must've stopped in to visit the Porters,' Nick said, making an accusation of it.

'I did, and the Duchess sent an apple pie along.'

'Yeah, I can smell the cinnamon — she's a good old gal, that one.'

The Duchess was one of the few people in this world Nick McCallum would ever pay even a grudging compliment. Rose Ann Porter was one of the only two people on the earth that could give Nick a task and have him do it, Rodeo being the other. Rodeo had taken Steamboat Bill's place in Nick's eyes. He was submissive to his big brother, though not always graciously so. Wynn and Kit virtually did not exist to Nick, outside of necessity.

'Did he ride all right?' Nick McCallum asked Wynn, nodding at the tarpaulin-covered wagon bed.

'He didn't make any complaints,' Wynn said coldly.

Nick either didn't hear the answer or care about it. He walked to the wagon bed and flipped the corner of the canvas tarp back to study the corpse lying there.

'Well, he's still dead, ain't he?' Nick McCallum commented.

'Yeah, and I didn't like driving from Rambler with him along. I was afraid someone was going to see him at the Porter place.'

'I told you not to stop anywhere,' Nick replied, stepping forward. As Wynn sat on the wagon's spring seat, watching, Nick opened the box and scooped at the pie with two fingers, tasting it.

'How is it?' Wynn asked. There was some censure in his voice. Nick, of course, missed it. It would not have mattered to him anyway. That was Nick; you had to take him as he was.

'Good, as always.'

'Fine. How about we get this gent buried now? I haven't enjoyed his company and I won't be sorry to see the last of him.'

2

'I told you it had to be done,' Nick McCallum told Wynn for the thirtieth time. The two men threw their shovels into the back of the wagon. The cold, lonesome mound of earth behind them was being folded in the dark shadows of the oak as day sank into evening.

'Yeah, I can see that,' Wynn replied — at least in Nick's mind it had to be done, the killing. He rested his forearms on the side of the wagon bed. 'But what's Rodeo going to say?'

'I wasn't planning on telling him,' Nick said, wiping a dirty cuff across his dirty forehead. 'You're the only one that needed to know.'

Yes, Wynn needed to know so that he could sneak over to Rambler Shack to recover the dead man, who Nick had not wanted to throw over his pony's back, seeing as he was in a hurry to get away last night after killing the stranger. Nick had also needed help with the burying. He figured that Wynn could get away from the McCallum ranch without being questioned by Rodeo.

Nick again offered his version of what had happened. 'Little guy like him, I didn't think he was going to level his Winchester on me. Little man, wearing spectacles . . . did you find those spectacles this morning, Wynn?'

'No,' Wynn answered. Nor had he found a Winchester rifle. No one would ever really know what had happened out there on the prairie except for the dead man and Nick McCallum, who had undoubtedly already convinced himself that his tale was the absolute truth. Nick had a habit of that, even as a boy. It made it hard to get the straight story from him; he became defensive, protecting his own truth.

The only thing that was certain was that Nick had killed some unknown man, for unknown reasons, far out on the range, distant from any town or habitation.

And the man had worn spectacles — where could these have gotten to? Certainly no wild animal would have taken them away. It bothered Wynn as he stepped aboard the wagon again. Bothered him, because those spectacles could lead to the identity of the man and lead to suspicions that he fallen victim to foul play. And there were only two ranches around for miles. The Porter place — and those two women could not be cast as killers by any sane person.

And the McCallum ranch.

Riding that handsome leggy roan of his beside the wagon, Nick looked free of any burden now that the evidence was planted in the ground. Wynn on the other hand was uneasy. He did not know who the stranger had been, what he was doing so close to their home range or why Nick had killed him. And Nick was never going to tell him or anyone else.

Certainly not Rodeo.

Nearing the stone house, Wynn

asked, 'Where's Kit?'

'I wouldn't know. He's probably eating his supper about now. What do you want to see him for?'

'The Duchess told me that she had given Kit a message for all of us.'

'Is that so? What's it about?'

'Have no idea,' Wynn shrugged. He slowed the wagon and turned it toward the barn. 'Something about there were going to be a few changes around here — Kit knows.'

'He's probably at the table. He just rode in from Gato Negro as I was leaving. The kid has it made with the ladies, doesn't he?' Wynn nodded glumly. Nick had swung down from his horse and was now walking toward the barn beside Wynn, leading his roan pony.

'Last time I was at Rose Ann's with him, that girl Becky just about came running when she saw it was Kit I was with. She didn't have eyes for anything else but him while we were there. How old is Kit anyway?'

'Seventeen, I think, no, make that eighteen.'

'That young? The kid is going to have a busy life,' Nick said. They entered the darkness of the barn and Nick began stripping his horse of its gear. 'And that Mexican woman — Alicia, is it? — Kit can't pass through that little Mex town without she starts fussing around, making him food . . . the kid is going to have a busy life! As long as he don't get in a fix where one of them Mexicans shows him what a knife is for.'

Wynn had never seen this Alicia himself, but both Kit and Nick had described her: bright, chocolate-colored eyes, ready smile. 'Put together as God had intended women to be built.'

Dropping the traces of the wagon Wynn only nodded sullenly. He was tired of hearing talk about Kit McCallum, Alicia and Becky Porter. He realized again that he was jealous of his younger brother.

What he needed to do now was to find Kit and ask him about the Duchess's message. Something was going to change, but what? Did she mean just on the Porter ranch or was it something that involved the whole valley? None of the McCallum boys liked the idea of change of any kind; they had things the way they liked them now and had a strong opposition to anyone stirring up things in any way.

Finished with unharnessing the blacks, he asked Nick, 'Want to go in to talk to Kit with me?'

'No. Whatever it is, I'll hear it sooner or later,' Nick answered reaching for the curry comb that hung from a nail on the wall. He did love to keep his sorrel gleaming. Scuffing his way toward the house, Wynn looked around, trying to see Rodeo at one of his favorite lookout posts, but could not find him. Neither was Rodeo's pinto pony tied up in front of the house. That meant that he and Kit were acting as watchers just now, for the house was never left unguarded. That had been one of Steamboat Bill McCallum's inflexible rules. 'I'd hate to come home and find a family of Indians having dinner around my table,' Bill had said in one of his lighter moods.

It was a simple fact that there was no one else around to watch home ground but the McCallums themselves. They owned very little, nothing really but the house and their small horse herd, and they could ill-afford to lose either. When the year grew shorter they would cull the horses and sell some to provide for their winter subsistence. When spring came again they would ride out on their adventures, but winter in Wyoming was no time for adventuring.

Kit was where Wynn and Nick had expected him to be — sitting back at the heavy wooden table, hands on his stomach, a much-depleted trencher in front of him. Wynn could see immediately what the meal had been: it was one of Alicia's frequent contributions to keeping Kit McCallum from starvation.

'Howdy, Wynn,' Kit said amiably. 'I would have saved you some, but I didn't know when you'd be back.'

'That's all right, Kit,' Wynn said,

pulling one of the heavy chairs out from the table. 'Mexican chow just don't heat up again worth a damn.'

'No, it doesn't. If there's a trick to it, I haven't learned it yet.'

Wynn could tell from what remained on Kit's platter what it had been. Rolled tacos. Corn tortillas with what seemed to be no more than a tablespoon of string beef sharing space with shredded yellow cheese, drowned in thick red salsa then rolled into tortilla tubes that were dusted on the outside with white cheese. There wasn't much to them, hardly enough to make a meal unless you ate them by the dozen, which Kit McCallum seemed to have done.

'The Duchess told me that she gave you a message for us — something about a few changes that were going to be made around here.'

Kit leaned back even farther in his chair and stretched his arms over his head. 'Oh, that,' he said. 'It's nothing to worry yourself about. It's just that the Duchess has decided that she needs to hire some men. Her horse herd has been growing and she feels guilty about having to ask us for help all the time. Like us, she means to sell off some of her stock before winter, and she'll need men to gather and drive them to market.'

'That's all?' Wynn asked.

'That's all. I told you it was nothing worth worrying yourself about.'

'Where'd she come across men worth hiring? Not in Collier, certainly.'

'No, she told me that they were men from down in Nebraska. The Guilefords, by name. It seems they know horses.'

'As long as they stay off our land,' Wynn said.

'And their eyes off our horses. I don't think there's much to worry about there — I've already told Rodeo what's up. He didn't seem too concerned. The Duchess will be sure to tell the new hires where our boundary is and make sure they know whose horses wear that big 'M' brand.'

'I suppose,' Wynn said reflectively. 'But those boys from out of the area might not respect the McCallum brand like local men, who know better than to tangle with Rodeo.'

And Nick. Rodeo was damned tough, and everyone knew it. Nick on the other hand was sneaky-tough, which made him just as dangerous, maybe more so. Nick hadn't killed a man — and what about the dead man? Was he one of Rose Ann's new crew? Had Nick already begun a war with the strangers?

'Who'd you say these new men were?' he asked Kit, who had risen and taken his Stetson from the row of wall pegs.

'The Duchess called them the Guile-fords. I don't know if they're all related or that's just what they call themselves. I never heard of no place in Nebraska called that, though I've only been there twice in my life.'

'Odd name,' Wynn said, following Kit to the front door.

'Is it? I suppose any name you never

33

heard before sounds odd. The Duchess said she only sent for three of them, couldn't see any sense in needing more cowhands, the size of her herd. So we don't have to worry about them.'

Kit obviously wasn't worried. He was of an age where he only worried about himself. What of Becky Porter? Weren't she or Rose Ann concerned with having a rough bunch of strangers on their ranch?

Well, that might have been only Wynn's own worries, his protective jealousy speaking.

Kit started off to relieve Rodeo's post at his rooftop watch. Before he left, Wynn asked, 'Tell me, Kit, does any of those Guileford boys happen to wear spectacles?'

Kit laughed and shook his head, 'Do you know any cowhand who does? Or who could afford them if he needed them? Where would he get them made? — Wynn, that is an odd question, isn't it? I've never yet had a look at any of them; as far as I know they're not on the Duchess's land yet. Why would you ask such a question?'

'I don't know — it's just something Nick suggested. I'm sure you'll hear about it after Nick has the chance to talk with Rodeo.'

Confess to him was more like it. Kit shrugged and started away again. Wynn started to the barn to recover his saddle mount. He thought that he should look around a little before darkness settled. After all, he conjectured, where there was one man with spectacles, there could be another lurking. There were a few unhappy omens mingled with the wind-tossed evening clouds as the Wyoming lands labored toward darkness.

3

Now, how many men there were for 500 miles around who wore spectacles? Dave Chandler wondered. Most of the men who did kept them at home on a desk or a book case, and were careful not to ride with them in the rough country where they could be lost; replacing them would be a long and costly business.

Yet here was a pair of gold-framed spectacles sitting in the mud out on this open-faced prairie with no sign of their owner in sight.

Chandler got to his feet, dusting the knees of his trousers with his free hand, holding the reins to his ugly piebald in the other. The horse chuffed and tossed its head, indicating to Dave that as far as it was concerned they had been halted here long enough, and it was time to be traveling.

It wasn't that bad an idea — but in which direction? Chandler had the gloomy thought that the broken spectacles were the only sign of Virgil Dodd that he would recover on the long prairie.

A shame — Virgil Dodd had been a hard-working, almost eager member of the territorial marshal's force. He had, in fact, volunteered to follow the Guileford boys north out of Cheyenne, when he could have waited a few days and gotten plenty of support from one of the roving posses.

'Hell,' Dodd had said, 'I've seen the worst of 'em, Tammany, he don't scare me — nor his cousins.'

'All right,' the captain had agreed dubiously. 'We can't let them get far away from us. Just find them, Dodd, assuming you can. Don't confront them, do you understand me?

'There's a telegraph line through to Collier now — use it! Send for help once you've located them. I don't mean to lose any more good men — or you

— to those damned Guileford boys.'

There was a smile on the captain's face as he said that, but it was a mighty thin expression. Virgil Dodd was a good man, small only in stature. He had a large heart and a whole bushel basket full of courage. He was good with the books in the office and also good in a stand-up fight as he had proven more than once. The captain thought that Dodd felt he had to keep proving himself because of his size — maybe he was right. It didn't matter, though; .44 Colts only came in one size.

They had no one else available to track the Guilefords after the bank stickup over in Medicine Bow.

So this was where eagerness led you? There being no grave and nothing to put in one, Dave Chandler kicked his boot against the hard Wyoming earth, fanning a little dust, and returned to his impatient piebald.

* * *

The Duchess sat in her rocker on the front porch of their little ranch house long after it had gotten too cool to sit comfortably. The clouds had risen in the west, taking on bunched indefinite shapes, and the wind from the north had picked up. Still Rose Ann sat in her old rocker, knitting needles clicking together as she watched the horizon and waited. Waiting — it was all she seemed able to do these days. With a sigh, the Duchess folded her knitting away and rose. Becky would need help with supper.

The task was complicated this evening by not knowing whether they were cooking for two or half a dozen. Rose Ann had compromised. She and Becky would have a hot roast beef dinner with boiled potatoes. If the Guilefords showed up soon enough they were welcome to share. If they arrived late they would have to be satisfied with beef sandwiches. Hungry off the trail, that would likely appeal to them as much as anything.

'No sign of them yet?' Becky asked, turning from the oven.

'Not yet,' Rose Ann said with another sigh, placing her basket of knitting aside. 'There's just the two of us eating again.'

Becky's sigh was not audible, but was issued with more force of feeling. She had wanted to invite Kit McCallum over to eat, but not knowing how many men would be there, Rose Ann had asked her to wait for another night. Becky moved dishes and pans around with more force than was necessary. She ached to see young Kit McCallum sitting down across the table, his ready smile lighting up the supper table.

'I thought the Guilefords were a reliable tribe,' Becky grumbled.

'That's what Tammany Guileford promised me when I met him down in Medicine Bow when I took the wagon down there to have that crooked axle re-slung. He seemed such a reliable old man himself that . . . ' Both women's heads came around. They had clearly

40

heard the sound of an approaching horse.

'I think it's only a single horse,' Rose Ann said, leaning forward to peer out the kitchen window.

A lone horseman! Becky's heart rate immediately rose. Could it be Kit McCallum?

'Likely they got strung out a way along the trail,' the Duchess speculated, 'or they have some men's long custom of always scouting out a place before riding into it.'

That could be, but the lone rider had now halted his horse, paused to tether it, and was now walking boldly up onto the front porch, his boot heels clacking firmly with each stride.

'It don't seem he's that wary,' Becky said. She let Rose Ann swish past her and lead the way to the front door where a light rapping continued. The Duchess signaled to Becky to stay back out of sight and she opened the door wide to the starry night.

A tall man stood silhouetted against

the night sky, hat in hand. Rose Ann tried: 'Mr Guileford?'

After a pause Dave Chandler replied, 'No, ma'am, my name's Dave Chandler. You'll have to forgive me for dropping by unannounced.'

The Duchess laughed. 'That's mostly the only kind of company we ever get, and few of them. Won't you come in and sit a spell?'

Dave was not surprised at the woman's hospitality. That's the way most folks were out on the land. He nodded his thanks and cross the threshold. He saw a pair of shy blue eyes peering at him around the corner, and he nodded at Becky as well. There was a sudden flare of crimson on her pale cheek and her face withdrew.

'Smells like I might have caught you at supper time,' Dave said. He stood still, his back to the cold fireplace.

'You did,' Rose Ann said, 'but that's all right. We were waiting for our menfolk, but they'll have to eat it cold if they don't get here soon.'

This last was only partially true. Hospitality was extended to everyone, but still when a young girl and a rough stranger were involved, the Duchess used a little caution with her welcome.

'Well, I guess then, I should see to my horse . . . '

'See to yourself first,' Rose Ann encouraged. 'You're welcome at our table if you have the time to stop and eat.'

'I surely have the time,' Dave said with gratitude. He had already adopted a scheme which seemed flimsy but had presented itself out of nowhere. 'I don't know when those darned Guilefords will get here. Maybe another day. I'm a cousin of theirs and was invited along, even though they didn't know how much help they'd need, if any.'

Dave and Rose Ann had seated themselves at the heavy table, leaving the serving to Becky, who had already lost interest in their conversation. She was unable to concentrate on much of anything these days — except Kit

McCallum. She knew that this afternoon she had treated Wynn a little shabbily, but that was only because she was caught in the depressing wake of not finding Kit arriving with him.

'Dave? That's your name, Dave Chandler?'

'That's it,' Dave acknowledged, removing his arms from the table so that Becky could serve him his platter of rare roast beef and boiled potatoes. A serving dish of butter and a steaming gravy boat were also placed before him.

'How is it that you arrived before the other Guilefords?' the Duchess asked.

'Well, ma'am, I expect most of them had work to catch up on. There wasn't nothing to do and not much point in doing it on our little postage-stamp spread. I got anxious to be moving.'

'Times tough down there?'

'I should say they are. That's why I was so eager to find any kind of work that might promise a few dollars.'

'A few is all it promises,' Rose Ann said. 'You act as if you don't even know why you're here,' she said, studying him by the candlelight.

Had Dave already tripped himself up without knowing it? He decided on honesty, or what he hoped would pass for it.

'I don't, and that's a fact. Tammany said there was plenty of time along the trail to fill me in — I guess I got impatient.'

'How did you know where to come?' she asked. Her eyes still held the shadow of a doubt.

'Can I say I didn't? I don't want you to take me for a complete fool. But there's so few ranches around here that I figured someone could tell me, and they did.'

Someone did all right — Virgil Dodd. He had done his job too well, it seemed, and caught up with the Guilefords. He could not tell anyone which Guileford had shot him, or even why those bandits were traveling this way.

'Yes, well, there's only the two spreads in this county,' Rose Ann said around a bite of beef. 'Us and the McCallums' Big M. There's four brothers living there and they have been a mighty help to us since my husband passed away.'

Dave was uninterested in the McCallums. He had never heard of them, being from down south, but he decided to let the lady ramble on. Sooner or later she would have to come back to the men he was interested in — the Guilefords, who had robbed the bank in Medicine Bow last week, killing a man during their escape, and now another man along the trail.

'Those boys are a pleasure to have around, aren't they, Becky?' Rose Ann asked and again Dave saw color rise in the girl's cheeks as she nodded an answer. Dave thought that the chances were that the girl was sweet on one of them.

'That's how I got around to hiring the Guilefords this year,' the Duchess was saying. 'I knew if I said anything about this year's roundup of our horses, the McCallums would generously offer to do it for us, to collect them and drive them to Collier to be sold. 'They're just that sort of men. But I know their herd has grown larger and they have their own responsibilities. I wanted to ask them for help, but it just wasn't right after all they've done for us.

'That's why I was so pleased when I met Tammany Guileford on my trip to Medicine Bow to have our wagon's axle fixed. I asked after working hands in the area and he told me that his own family would be pleased to hire on for the summer, droving horses. He said that they had all seen enough of Medicine Bow for a while and they would be happy to ride up and help us out.'

Dave thought that he would bet they had seen enough of Medicine Bow for a while after robbing that bank, and would be happy to be offered a hideout.

But how had Virgil Dodd gotten wind of this and managed to get ahead of the Guileford gang? Well, no one had ever said that the little man wasn't clever; this time, however, it seemed that he had outsmarted himself.

Finished with his meal Dave tried to make casual conversation and also gather information.

'Where do you have to drive your horses to sell them?' Dave asked.

'Well, Collier of course, it's the nearest town. We usually have buyers come through about this time of year. These men are long drovers, or have hired some. Our ponies end up in Montana, mostly, although we do send some in the other direction as far away as Arizona. All I care about is getting them off my property and paid for. That brings in enough money to buy a few things and stock up on food for the winter. Didn't you see any horse traders in Collier?'

'You know, I never did. I never saw Collier is what I mean. I must have swung wide of it.'

'I'll say you did, coming up from Medicine Bow — isn't that where you said you were from.' Her eyes had narrowed a little again, suspicion returning.

She was a shrewd woman and Dave knew better than to invent any complicated tales that might trap him.

'Usually folks plan on stopping at the last town they can find.'

'I might have, but the thing is, I didn't find it.'

'I see,' Rose Ann said thoughtfully. Becky was obviously bored. She asked her aunt if she might get up from the table and was given permission.

'I'm going to get some fresh air,' Becky said, reaching for a hooded coat.

'Keep an eye out for those arriving men,' Rose said. Becky said she would and the screen door shut lightly behind her.

'If Kit happens to ride over she wouldn't see the Guilefords if they came in blowing trumpets.'

'Kit?'

'Kit McCallum.'

'Is that the boy she favors?'

'Nobody said she did,' Rose replied a little tightly.

'No, but some of the signs are there.

Well, that's the way of the world, isn't it?' Dave changed the subject, 'Is Collier the only settlement nearby?'

'Now,' Rose Ann waved her hand in a vaguely easterly direction. 'There was a little town called Rambler out that way. It was doing all right when my husband first brought us here. The town was unwanted; the great country found it could well do without it. For a time there were six or seven houses there and a couple of shops, but the town could not support itself and there was no nourishment to be had from the long prairie. Little by little it blew away and was abandoned. There is still one house out there, or so they tell me. A snake-infested tumble-down affair. They call it Rambler Shack, its only use is as a point of reference.'

'I see, a dead town.'

'Cold dead. It happens to all things civilized, I suppose but that town had no chance.'

'Tough for those who put their work and hopes into it,' Dave Chandler said.

There were too many failed high plains towns and farms to even count. People went after their dreams with their hearts and left their brains behind. Anyway, it cleared that up — the Guilefords could not be holed up in Rambler Shack.

Where then were they, and how had Virgil Dodd come upon them and gotten himself killed?

Dave was relaxed now, speaking over rapidly cooling coffee. 'So unless someone meant to double back all the way to Collier, there's really no place to go but here and the McCallum ranch.'

'Who are you talking about?' Rose Ann asked, that hint of suspicion flashing again. Dave had asked the wrong question again.

'Just anybody who did not know the country well — like me.' He smiled but got none in return.

'Well, there's nothing to know north of Collier — if you don't count that Mexican town. Gato Negro, it's called. Know what that means, do you?'

51

'Black Cat,' Dave replied.

'Yes, but it's not some old pussy cat that it's named after. Those Mexicans tried driving sheep up from Mexico. Somewhere along the way a jaguar fell in with them, liking the possibility of having a good meal every day without even having to hunt for it. At the end of their long drive to Wyoming, that black jaguar had eaten or maimed about half of their flock, and not a few Mexicans.

'The surviving sheep didn't do well up here, the big predators took them easily.' She shrugged heavily. 'Just another idea that sounded good in the planning, turned into a disaster in the doing.'

'Like Rambler Shack.'

'Just like Rambler Shack.'

Dave found himself hoping for the women's sake that their plan to drive horses to Collier with the Guilefords didn't turn out to be such a large error in judgment. For a split second he thought of telling Rose Ann about these men. He decided not to. What about these McCallum boys of whom they spoke so highly? Perhaps they should at least be alerted? He decided not to discuss this with Rose Ann, but to see how things stood in the morning and make his decision then. At least there were some helpful neighbors around if the Porters needed them. Knowing that made it a little easier for Dave Chandler to sleep when he finally rolled up the hay in the barn loft.

4

'You don't mean to do any killing, do you?' Wynn McCallum asked his oldest brother across the heavy table where the smoky lantern glowed dully on used supper dishes.

'Of course not,' Rodeo replied. His face was as still and hard as carved walnut, his eyes as black and apparently unfeeling as any wild thing's. On this evening he had dampened his hair and combed it straight back. It was as if someone had tried to neaten up the devil.

'Unless it's necessary,' Nick McCallum put in almost eagerly. Nick had not removed his hat for dinner and now leaned forward at the table, hunched over his coffee cup.

'And that's always a possibility,' Kit said from his seat at the foot of the table. His eyes were bright as he studied

54

his older brothers intently. Kit idolized Rodeo and Nick, Wynn knew. Every word of Rodeo was an undisputed fact to him.

Such bloody gods to follow!

Rodeo began again, his black eyes on Wynn.

'It's never any good to involve a murder in your plans, it complicates things and can set a man to running.'

'Yes, it does,' Nick said too eagerly. Wynn wondered if he had yet informed Rodeo of the murder he had committed. He thought not, for at that moment Nick gave Wynn a sideways, inquiring glance. Nick said to Rodeo, 'I remember two years ago when you were on the run for three months.'

'I learned my lesson that time,' Rodeo said, 'but, no, there won't be any killing — there shouldn't be any need for it.' This calmed Wynn's concerns only a little. Both of his older brothers had their father's sense of correctness, and as little restraint.

Wynn found his thoughts drifting

— to the Porter ranch where the little white-haired girl was likely preparing for bed and thinking her own thoughts . . . Wynn looked at Kit McCallum at the foot the table and rose hastily, his hand setting his tin plate to clattering as he brushed it.

Rodeo looked his way without expression and went on. 'Saturday's the day the Eagle Eye and other assorted businesses ship their weekly take to the bank in Medicine Bow for safekeeping.'

'How do you know that?' Nick asked, earning him a scathing look from Rodeo.

'Bertha told me,' Rodeo replied as if Nick's question was not worthy of an answer. Bertha was a remarkably well-padded girl, who worked at the Eagle Eye. Rodeo favored her when he was in the mood, they all knew.

'How would she know?' Nick, who was not quite finished, asked. The look he got from his brother was as cold as an adder's this time.

'Nothing goes on at the Eagle Eye that Bertha doesn't know about,' Rodeo said. Then he got back to business.

'Saturday morning stage is the one that carries all of the coin. Nick and I will be in town. We'll watch the stage leave and then we'll follow it, fifteen minutes later. We'll ride right in its wake, so that no one will be able to pick out our back trail later. Since we can't lose the coach, we'll let them travel twenty, thirty miles on, then we'll stop it and unload it.'

'There's bound to be a shotgun rider on board with all that money,' Wynn objected. Rodeo twitched his lip a little, as if that were a slight annoyance to be dealt with later.

'We'll stash the money and then spend the night in Collier while the driver and the shotgun rider take a barefoot walk into Medicine Bow. By the time they get there Nick and I will just about be ready to rise, eat some breakfast, and ride out of Collier before a telegraph from Medicine Bow can be sent and Marshal Bleeker and whoever else he can rouse can even saddle their horses to ride after the coach.'

'Which won't matter because we'll be long gone,' Nick said.

'What'll I be doing?' Kit wanted to know.

'You'll be here,' Rodeo said evenly. 'The two of you — Wynn and you. When have we ever gone and left the place unguarded? You two work up your shifts as you like, but I want someone watching at all times, like always. When we reach home we have to find it as we left it.'

Kit started to respond, but as crestfallen as he felt at being left out of this adventure, he knew that Rodeo had already worked out the plans in his mind, and there was no point in trying to talk him out of or into anything else.

Wynn was not disappointed at being left out of the plan; in fact he was vaguely relieved. He had known that Rodeo was up to something since the winter gathering of their horses had begun. They were now collected in the pole corral where they would be kept until it was time to drive them into Collier. Their condition could be more closely assessed, and grain and dry hay given them to prevent grass founder. Big M did not sell less than prime horses; their reputation was important for future sales.

Wynn could see Rodeo, speculative and cool, regarding each horse that was driven in, wondering at its market price, measuring that price against their need to provide for themselves through a four-or five-month Wyoming winter.

Some of the herd must have come up short in Rodeo's eyes. Wynn had known by the look on Rodeo's face the last days of round-up that he had found the horses wanting and he would soon turn his hand to an 'adventure'.

'Well, we're left out again, brother,' Kit said to Wynn when the supper table had been cleared. Nick was now on the roof in one of their watching positions and Rodeo had gone to his bed to get some of the extra sleep he figured to need in the morning.

'Looks like it,' Wynn answered without concern.

'I don't think I'll get any proper chances until Nick gets himself killed. And he will, you know. The man's way too eager to go for his iron.'

'Isn't he?' Wynn said. Once again he wondered silently about the identity of the unknown man Nick had killed.

★　★　★

They hadn't awakened Wynn with their leaving, but looking out on this bright new morning he could see that, as he had expected, Rodeo's pinto pony and Nick's burnished roan were gone. He had known they would be; when Rodeo said that something was to be done, it always was. It was something he had learned at the knee of Steamboat Bill.

What was surprising was that Kit McCallum was up as well, and looking eager to ride. Was he going to defy Rodeo and ride after them? Unthinkable.

'Well,' Kit said cheerfully, 'you finally

crawled out of bed!'

The kid stood in the corner near the iron stove, finishing a cup of coffee.

'What do you mean — I'm not late, Kit. If anything you've risen early. Why aren't you up keeping watch from the roof?'

'Why?' Kit asked with that bright smile of his. 'I mean, you're here. Rodeo and Nick haven't been gone long enough to get themselves in any trouble. What problems could we have?'

'I guess you're right,' Wynn muttered, pouring himself a cup of tepid coffee.

'I decided to get myself some breakfast, that's all.'

Glancing around Wynn saw not an eggshell, no sign of bacon waiting to be sliced.

Kit laughed behind his back. 'Not here, you knucklehead!'

'What do you mean?' Wynn asked.

'I'm bound for Gato Negro now that you're up. You've never tasted Alicia's *huevos rancheros*. I tell you, that's a breakfast!'

61

'You're riding out this morning?' Wynn wagged his head slowly 'It's a bad day for it; Rodeo will raise hell.'

'How's he ever to know? No one's going to tell him.' Kit's eyes got as serious as they ever did. Wynn could only shake his head again.

'No. I guess no one ever will,' Wynn said. 'Still, Kit, I wish you wouldn't go over there'.'

'Brother, just because your whole world begins and ends with this ranch, it doesn't mean we all feel that way — especially not us younger fellows.' There was a light taunt intended and accepted. Wynn supposed Kit was right in his way, but if Rodeo ever found out . . .

It was best just to keep his mouth shut about Kit's escapades.

Within the hour Kit had ridden out on his pretty little tri-colored paint horse and Wynn was left alone, master of the Big M ranch. What now? He knew he should immediately take up the station on the roof of the stone house, but there was no one else around, meaning no one was there to make the morning round, checking on the penned up ponies in the pole corral and the cattle herd. However Rodeo's adventure worked out, losing these would absolutely cripple Big M.

Wynn spent some time arguing with himself, but he knew his own preference would win out, and it did. He would ride the ranch perimeter. Rodeo had been right to leave two men behind; he could not be in two places at once, something Kit either forgot or cared not about.

Wynn gobbled down his breakfast: biscuits fried in bacon grease followed with hot coffee, about the only morning meal Wynn knew how to whip up. Kit was a fair hand in the kitchen, but Kit was off in Gato Negro, stuffing his belly with a real cook's exotic concoctions. It was easy to understand Kit's appetite for Mexican food and Mexican maidens, but this was a critical time to be guarding the house; you'd think the young man would realize that.

If Kit had stayed at home, he could have taken a round of the Big M, which well could have included a short visit to the Porter place. Becky Porter would have been glad to see him. Wynn didn't understand his brother's preferences. He pondered that for a while until images of Becky became too heavy and he threw his plate and tin cup in the sink and went out to saddle the piebald.

It was an hour on when Wynn spotted a lone man riding a bay horse over the next fold in the hills, near to the cattle herd, and he lifted the piebald's pace in that direction, feeling some sense of urgency. No one should be riding the Big M range for any reason, and Wynn could not recognize horse or rider at that distance.

The only folk who ever rode their way were Marshal Jack Bleeker, who occasionally came by just to let the boys know he hadn't forgotten them, or a lost traveler. Once Kit had encountered a sad-faced man looking for his sister, who had written him that she was moving to a place called Rambler; and Rodeo had once come across two Mexicans trying to find Gato Negro. Rodeo had glared at them long and then flagged his thumb over his shoulder sending them south. These were rare and isolated cases — the local people knew well not to cross the McCallum land.

But here was a stranger idling his way in the direction of the house. True, the herds were far away, and there was nothing a lone man could bother or take out here, but Wynn thought the rider should be warned away. After all, he could have been one of the Duchess's imported horse drovers unsure of his way. Wynn decided to approach the man with a smile.

It was a tight expression.

Riding down the gentle slope of the grassy knoll, Wynn came upon the man simply sitting his horse, sipping at his canteen. The stranger nodded as Wynn approached. Lowering his canteen, the man said: 'Mornin'. Is your name Guileford by chance?'

'No,' Wynn replied, 'is yours?'

The stranger grinned. 'No, it's Dave Chandler, actually.'

'I'm Wynn McCallum,' Wynn said without offering his hand to the stranger. 'McCallum, which starts with an M. This is Big M range you're riding on, Chandler, and we'd prefer not having too many strangers around trampling our grass.'

Chandler appeared to take no offense. 'Wynn McCallum, is it? I've heard the good Porter woman speak highly of you — Becky too.'

'You know them!' Wynn asked with some surprise.

'I do. Not well, but I do,' Dave answered.

'What are you, some sort of relation?'

'No, I just stopped by looking for some men I've been trying to find. Look,' Dave said, tipping his hat back. 'I'd better be honest with you, Mr McCallum — it may be important to you and your brothers to know this. My name is Dave Chandler, as I told you.

I'm a deputy territorial marshal up from Cheyenne . . . say, mind if we step out of leather and sit a while? This may take some time to tell.'

They sat in the heavy shade of the gnarled old oak. Dave took time getting started, but he had come this way to warn the McCallums and so he told Wynn all he knew, truthfully. Wynn's expression didn't change much, but he was listening intently to every point. A lawman, was he? Wynn thought nervously about Rodeo and Nick, even now out committing robbery.

But Chandler had said he was up from Cheyenne. What could he want out here?

'There's a bunch of men from down near Medicine Bow who have somehow talked Rose Ann Porter into letting them stay on the Porter Ranch. All they are doing is hiding out while the law looks for them. Apparently she was told that they were horse drovers willing to help her with that work.'

'She always needs somebody to help

drive her horses to market. We've always been happy to help, but this year Rose Ann decided she was asking too many favors of us and wanted to hire her own summer crew.' Wynn paused, then asked seriously, 'I assume you're talking about the Guilefords. It's a name she mentioned, and you as well. What is it these Guilefords have done?'

'Robbed a bank down in Medicine Bow,' Dave told him. 'It was a sloppy job. They ended up killing a man on their way out of town.' His eyes lifted to meet Wynn's expressionless face. 'And it seems they murdered a deputy marshal who was chasing them, not a mile from here.'

Wynn's heart gave him one solid warning bump as he weighed this in the light of what he already knew. 'Where was this, did you say?'

'Over toward what's known as Rambler's Wreck.'

'You found a dead deputy?' Wynn asked, hoping his first judgment was wrong.

'No,' Dave answered, 'I never did find his body, but I found articles of his — these.' Dave reached into his inner vest pocket and displayed a bent pair of gold-rimmed spectacles. 'They belonged to Virgil Dodd: a small man, a dedicated man, and a friend of mine.'

'I guess you'd know,' was all Wynn could think to say. Inside he was cursing Nick McCallum, wondering at his own stupidity in helping dispose of Dodd's body. Was this deputy even telling him the truth, all he knew of the incident? 'So that's the Guilefords?' Wynn mused.

'Yes,' Dave answered, stretching. His every move was now under Wynn's close scrutiny though he did not show it. 'They're thieves and killers, and don't seem to care much who their victims are.'

'What did you tell the Duchess about them?' *And Becky.*

'I just told her I was a cousin to them. She doesn't know anything about the Guilefords at all.'

'Why come over here?' Wynn asked bluntly.

'Well, I guess I'd hope that if you boys knew who they were, you'd offer to the make the drive for her one more time. And, I felt that it was right for you boys to be informed that there's a gang of hard-cases in the area.'

'You're right, there, deputy,' Wynn said, rising to his feet. 'Except I really don't know what we can do to help Rose Ann Porter.' *And Becky.* 'You see it's time we were getting our own horse herd to Collier. The buyers will be there soon . . . ' He hesitated. He hadn't come out on the range this morning knowing he would have to invent excuses and lies for the law. 'My brother Rodeo is off the ranch just now — he's the one who would have to make a decision about helping the Duchess — if she needs it.'

'I think she will,' Dave said, 'I think she's about to lose her entire horse herd, don't you?'

'Can't the law do something?' Wynn almost pled. He didn't want to lay this problem at the foot of Rodeo . . . or

Nick, who only knew one solution to problems.

'Too far away,' Dave told him. 'Look — I'm not asking you boys to go charging in, guns drawn, but maybe if the Guilefords knew that this Duchess of yours had some strong neighbors, they would be willing to just pull out rather than fight over the little profit they stand to make from stealing a horse herd.'

'That's how you see it, is it?' Wynn asked.

'It was just a thought, a hope, maybe,' Dave Chandler said, his voice a little tight. 'I came up with it on the ride over. I have no idea what the Guilefords would do if you boys show up kind of casually. I have no idea of what might happen to the Porter Ranch horses, or to the Duchess and Becky if you don't.'

5

Wynn McCallum took a slow glum ride home through a gathering low mist. The dismal gray weather suited his mood exactly. He noticed as he approached the stone house that there was no sign that Kit had returned. There was no smoke curling up from the chimney; no one was visible on the roof. No horse stood in the stone corral, and when he took his piebald horse into the barn he saw no sign of Rodeo's pony nor Nick's roan. Of course, those two would not have returned from their adventure yet no matter how it had gone.

He stood for a moment in the doorway of the barn, looking through the drizzle toward the house. The day had started poorly and seemed to offer little hope of getting better. They now had a deputy territorial marshal watching the ranch. He — Dave Chandler

— had brought news that the Guileford boys were a bank-robbing crew with the law on their trail, and they had staked out the adjoining Porter Ranch as their hideout, possibly having it in mind to steal the Duchess's horse herd to boot.

Chandler had also brought the news that the man Nick McCallum had unthinkingly shot down was also a deputy marshal. Rodeo would not be thrilled to hear about a loitering lawman appearing on the heels of their attempt to stick up a stagecoach. He would be rightfully irate when the news of Nick's killing became known to him. If Kit had not returned before Rodeo's arrival it would only increase his fury. And just who, he would ask, was out watching the penned horse herd, or were they just planning on leaving these for the Guilefords as well?

It did not stand to reason, but Wynn figured that all of this would be seen as his fault. It would not be a nice surprise for Rodeo, no matter how his adventure had gone. And if it had gone badly,

Rodeo's rage would have no limits.

Wynn slogged toward the house, still holding the vague hope that Kit would be there to welcome him. He was not.

Miserably, Wynn poured himself a cup of nearly cold coffee, drank it, and climbed the pole ladder that led to the trapdoor that concealed the entrance to the roof.

He settled in the one-man shelter on the south side of the roof where he had full view of the Collier road and the trail to Gato Negro and kept his shivering, damp watch with no hope of relief and only miles of gloom to survey.

★   ★   ★

As Dave rode eastward, toward the Porter Ranch, he noticed a few stray horses here and there, and hied a few of those who were willing to move from their spots toward the Duchess's corral. He wasted little energy on the job. It didn't matter either way, he figured, but he had presented himself as a ranch hand and should at least pretend that was what he was.

The ground fog had deepened, thick and cold, and all that was visible were the very crowns of the scattered oak trees above the clouds. The reckoning was near, Dave figured.

Surely the Guilefords would show up soon, and he would have to explain his presence there. He had told the women that he was a cousin, but of course none of the Guileford bunch would recognize him or even know his name. Was there a way out of this besides telling the truth and shooting it out with a gang of armed men? Probably not — but he thought he might just give it a try. It depended on the women's wits and nerve, and their inclination.

Dave Chandler regretted now not telling the women before about the Guilefords, but there was no going back. Besides, would they have even believed him?

It was too late for doubts and recriminations now, for standing in a row in front of the Porter house as

Dave emerged from the fog, was a group of three horses, two a dark gray in color and one which had tried to be white and just missed. Three horses tethered in a row; that meant three men inside the house. The time had come — he could either face the Guilefords or remain on his bay horse and ride out of there as fast as he could. He went with the third plan, the one which was utterly dependent on the Porter women.

As luck had it, Becky Porter was standing on the small front porch, wrapped in a dark blue shawl. Taking a deep breath, Dave rode directly that way. He called out, 'Mornin', Becky!'

She turned to peer at him through the grayness of the day. When she had hesitated uncertainly long enough, he added, 'Just rode over from the ranch to see if everything was all right. The other boys will be along by and by.'

Becky recovered herself enough to say, 'Oh, it's you, Dave. You were just a ghost coming out of that fog.'

'Didn't mean to scare you. It's just

me, Dave Chandler.'

'Well, step down, Dave. Aunt Rose has company in the house just now.'

'Company?' Dave asked as he swung down. Becky had caught on to the fact that they were playing a small game now, though she didn't understand it all. She hoisted her shawl up over her head where her pale, fine hair was pasted by the dampness of the day.

'Maybe I'll come back another time,' Dave suggested, but Becky shook her head vigorously, her eyes wide, frightened.

Dave asked, 'Maybe you can show me that broken beam on the hayloft. I can't remember what size we'll need for that job. I think I'd better measure it to make sure we have one long enough on hand.'

'I'll show you,' Becky said. She stepped hastily off the porch and started for the barn, Dave following in her tracks, leading the bay.

She was shuddering when she halted inside the gloomy barn, and wasted no time in telling Dave, 'I don't like these men, Dave. I'm afraid of them. I was hoping you really were one of the McCallum boys — even Nick.'

'I told Wynn what was up; someone will be along sooner or later.'

'Didn't you talk to Kit?' she asked hopefully, but already disappointed with the expected answer.

'Wynn was the only one I talked to. I didn't see any of the other boys around, though they might have been.'

'Dave,' Becky said, taking hold of the fabric of Dave's damp flannel shirt, her eyes searching his placid blue eyes, 'these men — the Guilefords — they're awful. One of them — a man called Gent, the one with the brushy gray mustache — he orders Aunt Rose around as if he's in some saloon, demanding coffee and liquor — of which we have none.

'That man in the black suit, Tammany, seems to be their boss. He's a little too slick for me, and that Darby. He's narrow, lanky. He barely moves in his chair, but his eyes follow me everywhere. He makes my blood run cold. I'd rather have a tea party with Nick McCallum. However did you meet these men?'

'I never have,' Dave Chandler said. 'Your description of them is the first I've ever heard.

'Then how . . . ?' Her hand dropped from his shirt sleeve and she took a step away, looking up at Dave doubtfully. He was going to have to tell Becky too. He wasn't much good as an undercover operative, it seemed.

He palmed his badge from his inside vest pocket, and showed it to the girl.

'That's a bad bunch in there, Becky, I've come tracking them for a bank robbery and a murder they did down in Medicine Bow. I pretended that I was their cousin so the Duchess would let me stay around waiting for them.'

'How did you mean to do anything against those three?'

'I don't know,' Dave was forced to admit, 'I just know I was going to try something. On their way they also killed a friend of mine, another deputy, out near Rambler's Wreck.'

'I see,' Becky said thoughtfully. Her eyes brightened. 'But there's a chance now, isn't there — now there's five of you, or will be when the McCallum boys arrive.'

'If they get here,' Dave said.

'Oh, but they will!' Becky assured him. 'You don't know what good friends they have been to us.'

'Then, I wouldn't want them getting shot on what is my job and none of their own.'

'Neither would I!' Becky said emphatically. 'But you won't be able to stop them, no one could! Kit will be in a fury, and nothing will stop Rodeo from coming to our aid.'

'And the other two?'

'Nick will follow after Rodeo wherever he leads — he's like a dog at his brother's heels.'

'And Wynn?'

'Oh, yes, of course Wynn will have to come if the others do.' There was some disparagement in her tone when speaking about Wynn. Dave did not understand it, but he was an outsider here, trying to learn only enough to be able to formulate some workable plan.

If it could be done.

★   ★   ★

Wynn McCallum was growing sleepy at his rooftop perch. He had dared to leave his outlook point twice already to pour a cup of coffee for himself, there being no one to ask for one. But it had done little to stir him to alertness. The coffee in the pot was gone now, and he didn't think he should take the time to boil another quart.

Rodeo and Nick were due to return soon, but there was no telling if they would be bearing loot and grins, or dragging in wounded and weary, or even pursued by an angry mob.

Of Kit there was no sign. Perhaps, with his belly full of warm cooking he was snuggled up somewhere wasting the day away. He had to know that if he didn't get home soon Rodeo would be there to read him the law from the Book of Steamboat Bill. But Kit was young enough to act negligently even in the face of Rodeo's wrath so long as he had his comforts at the moment. There was tomorrow and there was today. In Kit's world tomorrow was something only to be considered when it arrived.

Something formed a shadow beyond the rank of fog-strangled oak trees surrounding the house and then darted away even as Wynn started to shoulder his rifle. A deer, only a deer.

The gray damp of the morning fog slid past heavily, and brought with it a sort of ghostly unease. Wynn was not a nervous man, but this weather was drawing on his composure. Leaves and small animals became enemies moving through the creeping fog. It reminded Wynn of when he was a boy and they withstood their last Indian attack. Steamboat had been with them still, and one could look at his face and see only indomitability. It was impossible to be afraid in the old man's presence. It was the being alone that did it, Wynn decided. Rodeo was not there with his sure hand and grim face, nor Nick, recklessly impatient, not Kit with his careless grin. Only Wynn whose patience had reached its limit.

There was that and that fact that he had a bunch of men — how many he did not know — who had come upon their land, bringing their reputation for murder with them.

And they had dragged along the law, maybe to meet Rodeo and Nick on their return home from adventuring.

Yes, it was a dismal morning. He shifted his body and sat with his back against the parapet for a while, thinking of another place he could be at on that morning . . . but she would not have cared much to see him. Becky only had eyes for the dashing young Kit McCallum.

★　★　★

'No,' said the Duchess, who had caught onto the game although Dave had not found the chance to explain everything to her yet, 'that was my mistake.' She laughed lightly, unconvincingly, keeping fearful eyes on Tammany Guileford.

'You see,' she continued, 'I had never met Dave Chandler before, and I knew he was coming up to help those boys, but I got things all muddled up when I saw him and mistakenly thought he was with you. I guess that's what happens as you get older.'

Tammany Guileford did not contradict Rose Ann; he didn't know enough to do so, but neither did he believe the Duchess's story. It made no sense whichever way she told it.

'Only a little confusion — it happens to me sometimes,' Rose Ann said, pursuing belief in Tammany's eyes.

Dave stood in the corner of the room, his hand never far from his Colt revolver. Of course, he did not wish to start a gunfight under these circumstances, but you never knew what might get into the minds of the Guilefords. They had shown themselves to have little restraint in using their guns.

'We'd better start planning the round-up, hadn't we?' Rose Ann asked shakily.

Tammany declined to answer. It was obvious, at least to Dave, that he was still wondering who Dave Chandler was. Any man unknown to the Guileford bunch was suspect to them. Still Tammany was hesitant to start a ruckus; who knew, the McCallum boys might be arriving at any time. It was best to wait and see how things played out for the time being.

'Well,' the Duchess asked Tammany, 'wouldn't you like me to sketch out a little map of my property and where my herd is apt to be?'

'It would be helpful,' Tammany agreed, his eyes still on Dave. Of the other two Guileford men, Leonard Gent seemed to have nothing to say except to ask when supper would be ready. The third Guileford, Darby, was also silent. His eyes continued to follow Becky Porter hungrily.

'Your ponies all branded, are they?' Tammany asked.

'Yes, they are,' Rose Ann told him, 'except for the very young horses which aren't old enough to make that drive this year.'

'I seen a few with a pyramid brand this morning,' Leonard Gent put in.

'I did too,' Tammany said. 'Is that your brand, Mrs. Porter — a pyramid?'

'Yes, we haven't bothered using a road brand on them this year as my herd is going alone. There shouldn't be any other brand on the place unless a Big M pony has wandered off its range.'

'Big M — that would be . . . ?'

'McCallum,' Dave said, as a loyal cousin would.

'Rodeo has probably already finished with his round-up and has them penned up to be examined and grained, while they watch for the occasional stray. That's his usual pattern.'

He looked at Dave sharply, but the Duchess answered for him.

'Why 'Big M'?' Gent asked with a

little sneer hovering about the question.

'That started many years ago when Steamboat Bill was still working his ranch. He ran across some bootstrap cattlemen that were about to slap their brand on one of his calves, taking it for a dogie. They said they didn't see the brand it already carried, since it was so small, so after some squabbling, Bill sent them off.

'Bill brooded over that for some time, and the next spring he had his calves branded with a double-sized 'M', saying they'd darn well see that one, and from then on the McCallum stock has always carried a big M brand — as notice to any near-sighted rustlers.'

Dave would have bet that the encounter involved a lot more than a casual warning, but the answer the Duchess gave satisfied the Guilefords, who had already lost interest in the subject.

'Don't know where the boys could be,' Dave said walking to the small front widow where he peered out.

'Maybe they ain't comin',' Gent said,

brushing his gray mustache with his fingers. He seemed to take that remark as a sly one.

'Oh, they'll be here if they said they would,' the Duchess said, 'you can count on that.'

Her face was now drawn; her usual cheerfulness seemed faded in the light of their suspicion. She managed to smile, however. Becky came briefly to the window to stand beside Dave, who seemed to be a comfort for her in this room full of killers.

'Maybe I should ride over to the McCallum ranch and see what they're up to,' Becky said hopefully.

'You can't be out riding the range on your own,' the Duchess said.

For a moment the Duchess's eyes swept over silent Darby Guileford — the man with the intent hungry eyes.

'No,' Dave said, 'but it is about time to see what's going on. I'll ride over with Becky.'

Gent had lost interest in the conversation again. He turned sharply in his chair to face Rose Ann. 'When do you think you'll get around to making my supper!'

Rose Ann, annoyed but not flustered, said, 'Just as soon as I can.' She looked at Becky. 'You and Dave better get going; go get some riding clothes on, Becky.'

Darby's eyes lit up with a wolfish gleam; perhaps he was thinking of Becky changing from her dress to denims.

'I'll feed these men,' Rose Ann said, 'meanwhile, try to find the McCallum boys. I want them to all come over and meet the Guilefords. If everyone is going to be out there scrambling around pushing horses in, let's make sure everyone knows friend from foe.'

Dave already had a pretty good idea of who was who. He looked the three Guilefords over, wondering which one had shot down little Virgil Dodd on the trail. He thought for a second of dangling the gold-rimmed spectacles in front of them, but thought better of it. Besides, if Virgil had been shot at a distance, they might never have even noticed that he wore them. They might not remember the little man, but Dave Chandler would make sure that they remembered the crime.

When it was time. Right now it would be foolish, dangerous if not suicidal, to confront the Guilefords. That would have to wait until he had some strong back-up behind him. Right now he could only stand his ground and hope the McCallum boys arrived before he had to set off in search of them.

*   ⋆   ⋆

Wynn McCallum was out of coffee, patience, and nearly of the well-worn dreams he always carried concerning Becky Porter. He was finished reciting the few poems he knew, tired of the simple mental games he had been playing. He was cold, and he had no doubt that his younger brother was somewhere warm and cozy.

He was tired of cursing Kit. He thought he would almost welcome an Indian attack though the land had been free of hostiles for almost twenty years Something — anything! — that would bring his weary body to alertness.

He heard the fog-muffled clopping of approaching horses and snapped to vigilance. Rising on numbed leg, Wynn rushed toward the north wall, rifle in his hand. Coming in from the north! Then it could not be Rodeo and Nick unless they had circled wide to avoid a following posse. It was not Kit, because there were definitely two horses making their way toward the house through the gray cotton-candy strands of fog spun between the oak trees.

Who then?

6

Becky Porter bounded down the inside stairs of the Porter house wearing a white blouse and leather jacket, blue jeans, and western boots, her hair knotted loosely at the nape of her neck. She looked to Dave, 'Are you ready?'

'Sure — you want me to saddle your horse?'

'No, I'll do it. He knows my hand.'

She, it seemed, was in an uncommon rush, perhaps because the crooked figure of Darby Guileford had lifted itself from the chair and now stood watching her and Dave; perhaps she was only in a hurry to see Kit McCallum again. It occurred to Dave that women did have a lot of things to think about, most of them concerning men.

They walked toward the barn, Becky looking back over her shoulder. Like an irritable, offended dog, Darby stood there in the mist, watching after them. 'He wants to go along,' Becky said in a wavering whisper.

'He won't; I'll promise you.'

Her voice remained in a whisper as they entered the dark barn. She stopped Dave and took his arm at the elbow. 'That man — he plans to follow us!'

'I know he does.'

'If he ever tries that, he'll find himself in more trouble than he can handle.'

'I believe you,' he said, although in truth he had no idea what the McCallum boys were made of.

She paused again, briefly. 'Can you use that Colt of yours, Dave?'

'I've never won a ribbon at shooting, but yes, I get along with it.'

'What about *him*?' she asked, motioning with her chin toward Darby Guileford.

'I have no idea, but he's an outlaw — most of those boys at least think of themselves as being good.'

'Because I was thinking . . . '

'Don't even waste time thinking

about it. If he pursues us, we'll be out on the open plains where he can't follow recklessly, and by the time he could even catch up with us, we'd be in sight of the McCallum house. I don't think he's got the nerve for that, unless he's plain crazy.'

'He may be,' Becky said quietly. 'You know, Dave, I think he just might be.'

Darby might have been. Dave had never ridden with him, but he had met a few who were crazy, and outlawed simply because they could not behave as normal people did. They would gun down a man for the fun of it, set fire to a crowded saloon over some implied snub, ride crazily at a group of armed deputies, which Dave considered to be a challenge to death they could not win and maybe did not even to wish to. They plain did not care enough about life to think it worth saving.

He shoved those thoughts aside within minutes as they found themselves out riding free on the plains, which were still shrouded with ground fog. Dave did not care for the fog. It had obscured the sight of what he thought had been Darby Guileford strolling to the barn where his own horse was kept.

'How many of the McCallum boys are at home?' he asked Becky. 'I saw only Wynn.'

'There will be more than that. Kit told me once that they never had less than two men standing watch at the house.'

'Do they not?' He folded his eyebrows. And why was that? It was a very suspicious behavior for honest men. And where was he leading this young blonde? Whether to safety or into a pot boiling with yet worse troubles he could not even guess at. They trotted their ponies on in shadowy silence toward the Big M ranch, Dave Chandler's thoughts as murky and cold as the rest of the world.

'There's someone standing on the roof,' Dave said as they neared the stone house. 'He's waving to us. It looks like Wynn.'

'It is,' Becky said, waving in return, 'It looks like he wants us to come ahead.' There was some surprise in the girl's voice. Dave looked at her for an explanation. 'I know you'll think this is strange, but in all the years we've known the boys, I've never been invited into their house.'

That was strange, but Dave considered it could be a reluctance on the part of the bachelor brothers to see the way they lived. It could be most anything, yet it was a little unusual, to say the least. Maybe, Dave thought, it was only his own lawman's way of looking at everything with suspicious eyes. Becky showed no suspicion or reluctance to proceed. With a glance behind her, she slapped her boots to the flanks of her sorrel, nudging it forward.

Wynn, with a rifle dangling in his hand, was there to welcome them when they circled into the dry front yard. His eyes flashed once to Dave Chandler and then settled themselves warmly on Becky.

'Who's with you?' Becky asked, knowing the ways of the ranch.

'No one,' Wynn answered with a smile that did nothing to conceal his anger. She took it to mean he did not wish to discuss matter further, and she was right. Even so, Becky eagerly examined the door and the front windows with her eyes, as if they might reveal a glimpse of Kit McCallum.

'Mind if we swing down?' Dave asked.

Wynn's mind had been elsewhere. 'No, of course not,' he answered, somewhat flustered. 'Please forgive me.'

Dave nodded, stepped out of leather and stood for a long minute looking down his back trail. He asked Wynn, 'You didn't see anyone behind us from up there, did you?'

'No.' Wynn still seemed flustered as he studied the trim little Becky Porter. 'Was there someone else?'

Becky answered: 'We — I — had the idea that one of Guilefords might try to follow us. The one named Darby. It might just be because he's so apart from everyone else, and you can't read a thing in his eyes. Sort of like . . . ' She was going to say 'sort of like Nick', but she stilled that observation before it could reach her lips.

'Maybe I ought to get back up on the roof,' Wynn said.

'I don't see the point in that,' Dave told him. 'You already know he's likely coming, and you must have good sight lines from inside the house.' Besides, Dave thought Wynn McCallum looked bone-weary. Had the man slept at all last night?

Wynn led the way to the door of the stone house with some reluctance. If someone was approaching the house he could not leave Becky standing outside. He grabbed the latch string, gave a short hard jerk, and let his visitors precede him into the interior of the house.

Dave stopped and took a look around the dark room they found themselves in. The room was cold, of course

— stone walls do very little to transfer the heat of the sun, and it was not what could be called a warm day outside anyway. Dave walked directly to one of the opposite slit windows, Wynn watching him uncertainly, and peered out. 'He's not there that I can see — but there is a free roaming horse out there in the oak grove.'

'Is it one of ours?' Wynn asked with some concern.

'It is,' Dave Chandler answered. The double-sized Big M brand on the pony's hip was easy to read even at this distance. The little blue horse lifted its head and looked in their direction, perhaps having heard human voices.

Wynn leaned forward farther to have a better look. 'I don't know what it's doing out there by itself.' Then, 'God! If the ponies have busted out of their pen, Rodeo will kill me.' After a few distraught moments' consideration, Wynn calmed himself. 'It's just a stray we missed on our sweep of the range. Sometimes one wanders down into the coulee and it'll take it awhile to find its way back up. It's just a stray,' he repeated as if trying to convince himself. 'I'd know the horse if it was one we drove into the pen.'

'I only see the one,' Dave said, trying to ease Wynn's concern.

'You don't understand,' Wynn complained, turning to stand, his back against the wall.

'I think I do,' Dave said placidly.

'You don't know my brother. I think I should go and check the holding pen.'

'You've already determined that the blue roan is not an escapee — he's probably trying to find a way to get *into* the pen — just hungry and lonely. If you did have a break-out, Wynn, there's not much you could do about it alone.'

'I know that, damn it!' Wynn said, flaring up. He looked with embarrassment at Becky and then deliberately clamped his jaw, turning away from her. He muttered something unintelligible under his breath.

Becky's face showed only concern,

not disapproval. 'But where's Kit — isn't he supposed to be here?' This time when she asked it seemed to be with sympathy for Wynn, not just out of her own desire to see the youngest McCallum boy. Dave listened because it was of concern to him as well, but Wynn did not answer. His thoughts were diverted.

'Someone's coming,' Wynn said. Looking toward the front door and listening more closely. 'Two horses.' Relief and dismay alternated on his face.

'It's Rodeo,' Wynn said, moving toward the door and throwing it wide. 'I know that shambling gait of his pinto, but ... where's Nick? That high-stepping red roan is easy to make out as well, but the second horse isn't the red pony.' Perplexed, Wynn McCallum stood, rifle in hand, peering into the gray tangle of the foggy day.

Dave had walked that way as well, Becky's heels clicking along behind him. Dave had no good feelings about this. There were too many cautioning signs about these men to ignore. There was no time to review these as out of the fog two ghostly riders appeared, riding from the oak trees. The taller man led the way. Riding a heavy pinto horse he looked toward the house with what seemed to be a silent caution.

The smaller man, dressed all in black save a white scarf, barely looked up as he made his way toward the stone house astride a buckskin horse. He sat awkwardly on his horse, like a man terribly uncomfortable in the saddle. Or like a man who was . . .

'He's hurt. Nick's bad hurt!' Wynn McCallum blurted out, rushing forward.

Nick McCallum's buckskin pony shambled its way into the yard; the pony was obviously exhausted. The pinto horse was little better off as its grim-faced rider guided it their way. Rodeo McCallum swung down from the saddle showing signs of a long trail behind him and snapped at Wynn, 'Give me a hand, will you? Nick's hurt and we've got to get him inside.'

For a moment Rodeo paused, puzzled by the appearance of Becky Porter and an unknown man, but he let it go for the time being and shifted around to take Nick from the buckskin's saddle, Wynn helping his brother with the effort.

'What happened?' Wynn asked, taking his share of Nick's weight on his shoulder.

'Nick's roan stepped in a prairie dog's hole, broke its leg, and rolled on him. We bought this buckskin from a farmer and rode on. I think Nick's got a broken rib.'

Rodeo said this between puffs of effort as he and Wynn, one under each arm walked an obviously wounded Nick McCallum into the house.

'Gee, that's tough,' Becky Porter commented to Dave as they followed the McCallum boys in.

'Yeah, it is,' Dave Chandler agreed. It was obvious that Nick McCallum was suffering greatly. It was equally obvious to Dave that Rodeo was lying through his teeth. They levered Nick onto the leather sofa where he sprawled half seated, half tilted toward the arm, chasing away anyone who offered to straighten him with a growl.

The man was in terrific pain, that was obvious. When Becky repositioned him despite his objections Dave caught a glimpse of the blood on his shirt. It was not caused by a broken rib, of which Dave had himself suffered a few.

There was a smear of spreading blood on his back, but on the front of his shirt was only a single puncture mark with only a little blood showing, and around that hole was the telltale singe of gunpowder.

Nick McCallum might have a broken rib, but it had been broken by a slug crashing through his body. Dave didn't know what the McCallum boys had been up to, but it was a good bet it wasn't looking up horse traders in Collier.

'Where's Kit?' Rodeo asked Wynn.

The older brother shot hard glances toward the trap door, which led to the roof. It seemed that Rodeo already knew — perhaps because they had seen no guard when they rode in. That seemed to be Wynn's thinking as well; he braced himself for the dressing-down which was sure to come.

Rodeo said, 'I asked you a question, Wynn. I'm not going to stand around while you take your time figuring how to answer me.'

Wynn let out a long breath and answered as if it physically pained him. 'Kit went to Gato Negro,' Wynn told the stone-faced Rodeo.

'He did, did he, and left you all alone at the house?' Rodeo did not raise his voice, but looking at Wynn you would have thought he'd been whipped. Wynn slowly, heavily nodded his head. Kit had violated the prime rule of the house.

'When's he coming back?' Rodeo asked.

'I don't know; he didn't say.'

Rodeo stared at Wynn in disbelief for a long while. 'Is this the way you're going to manage Big M if something happens to me?'

Wynn didn't even attempt to respond to that; Rodeo was not expecting an answer. Nick groaned heavily and all eyes shifted that way for a moment.

'I can wash the wound out and bind it up,' Becky offered, 'but I'll have to cut his shirt away.'

'Do whatever you can do, Miss Porter,' Rodeo said. 'While you're at that maybe you can tell me just what you're doing over here.' Rodeo's obsidian eyes took in Dave Chandler as well. 'And who this is.'

'I can tell it easier,' Wynn believed. 'Do what you can for Nick, Becky.'

Rodeo seated himself on the black leather couch beside his wounded brother. 'Just so she's not waiting for Kit,' Rodeo snapped, 'because he won't be coming home no more.'

'Never?' Wynn asked, his expression one of astonishment.

'Not to stay, certainly. The kid made his choice and it endangered all of us.' Rodeo paused, looked directly at Dave, and said, 'Tell me all, Wynn. You might as well start by introducing me to your friend there.'

'It's kind of complicated, Rodeo. If you'll let me just ramble through it . . .'

'That's what I'm asking you to do, Wynn. First things first — I asked you explain why you let this lawman into this house.'

7

Wynn started, and flashed a look at Dave, which found its way back to Rodeo McCallum.

Obviously Wynn was wondering how his brother could have known that Dave was a deputy marshal. Rodeo smiled just enough so that they could tell that was what the expression was meant to be.

'A lawman walks a certain way,' Rodeo said, 'watches a man a certain way — hell, he smells a certain way and I can smell lawman all over this one.' Rodeo did not speak in a manner that was meant to be offensive, and Dave took no offense.

'But . . . ' Wynn was flustered again. 'Dave's all right. If I can just get through my story once.'

Dave was grateful for Wynn's vote of confidence though he knew it would do nothing to change Rodeo's opinion. But Rodeo nodded. Wynn could have his say. However, before he could begin, there was another pained groan from Nick. Becky had removed his shirt and now had to force Nick to hunch forward as she tried to wrap his still-bleeding torso with white linen. Rodeo looked up sharply.

'Before you get started, Wynn,' Rodeo said. 'Do you mind telling me what this girl is doing here? Not looking for Kit?'

'No,' Becky Porter said sharply. The glare in her eyes was almost savage. 'Not that!' She tied another rough knot in the linen bandage. The medicine cabinet of the McCallum boys had been stocked full with rolled bandages, carbolic, surgeons' waxed thread and needles, cotton, iodine, and other incidentals. Every rancher tried to keep a stock of such things on hand, but to Dave Chandler's eyes their supply seemed excessive.

'She came with me mostly for her

own protection,' Dave said. 'She didn't feel safe with the Guileford gang in her house.'

'What gang? Guilefords; who the hell are they?' Rodeo demanded. 'You say they've taken over the Duchess's house?'

'Now, can I tell you?' Wynn asked.

'Please do.'

Wynn did so, making a fairly cohesive tale out of a situation which might have seemed convoluted but was basically a simple matter of coincidence. That is, the Guilefords had arrived in the area on the very afternoon Rodeo had planned his stage holdup. Dave, who had been tracking the Guileford boys, had accidentally inserted himself in the happenings.

Only Rodeo, who knew all about his own affairs, could understand the whole story.

'They've got the Duchess prisoner in her own house?' Rodeo said with savagery. He found another rifle in the gun cabinet. 'I'm going over there. Wynn, you're going with me. No one can do that to my neighbor, especially not a nice woman like the Duchess.'

On the couch Nick McCallum mumbled something and struggled mightily to try getting to his feet.

'What's he saying?' Dave asked Rodeo.

'What do you think? He said he's going with us.'

Dave studied the man, bare-chested, blood soaking the new bandage, and said, 'He can't go. Look at him! He'll be lucky if he doesn't bleed to death along the trail. You've got to tell him 'no'.'

Rodeo turned hot eyes on the deputy marshal. 'You tell him; I won't. He's a McCallum man and he means what he says. You can stay here and watch the girl.'

'No,' Dave said. 'Uh-uh. Listen, Rodeo, I don't know how this is going to work out, but I'm the man who has the papers on the Guilefords. If one of them should get killed, I can prove it

111

was in the rightful pursuit of bank robbery suspects. With me along, everything you do shines; on your own, it will look like range justice. You have that much time to be wasting it in jail right now, do you, Rodeo?'

Rodeo McCallum frowned, looked toward the door, toward Dave Chandler and at the bare-chested Nick McCallum, who had managed to rise to his feet from the couch with Becky's help.

It was Becky who spoke in a quiet, determined voice. 'I'll stay right here, Rodeo. You boys do what has to be done for Aunt Rose Ann.'

'Don't you let anyone in,' Rodeo instructed her with a brotherly sternness.

'Not an insect,' she promised.

'Nick,' Rodeo said, looking at his brother who was weaving on his feet, perspiring. 'I wish . . . '

'Oh shut up, Rodeo,' Nick said. 'Somebody might have it in mind to hurt the Duchess. Let's ride while I still can be of some use.'

All three of the McCallum brothers were determined not to let anything befall Rose Ann Porter, especially Nick. If Rodeo was all his father's son, Nick seemed deeply devoted to his mother whom he could not have known well, and now to the Duchess. Both of these two men took the time to switch horses while Wynn saddled his bay horse again. Dave Chandler's pony was tired, but relatively fresh. It had not been ridden hard or far on this morning.

Wynn was the first done and he stood in the doorway of the barn, talking to himself. He did not muffle his thoughts as Dave emerged from the barn leading his alert little piebald pony.

'It makes no sense,' Wynn McCallum was muttering as he looked toward the stone house. He glanced at Dave as the lawman led his horse forward. 'Kit has that little girl all corralled, and here she is just waiting for him.'

'Love is strange,' was all Dave could think to say.

'And Kit's not here,' Wynn said,

admitting Dave to his conversation. 'The girl is smart, very pretty, both trusting and needful, and Kit McCallum . . . '

'You said he's got another girl,' Dave said, swinging into his saddle.

'Well, he does,' Wynn admitted. 'A pretty little Mexican girl. She cooks for him, and from the glow in her eyes when Kit's around, I think she'd curry and shoe his horse for him if he asked her to.'

'Well,' Dave commented as the group of four started toward the Porter ranch, 'it seems that Kit prefers this Spanish girl to Becky. Sometimes things just work out that way and it's hard to explain them.'

'It wouldn't be hard for me to explain,' Wynn said. 'Becky Porter is a wonderful girl. I'd be proud to have her. Any man would.'

'But there's always Kit,' Dave said.

'There's always Kit. Dave, I don't think the girl even sees me when Kit's around, and I'd never intentionally come between Becky and Kit, not as much as she seems to care for him.'

'I suppose you'll just have to wait your chance,' Dave Chandler said.

'I'll wait, Dave. Rodeo is talking tough about keeping Kit from the house. And Rodeo isn't a man for idle talk. Maybe now, with Kit staying away . . . but I don't think Becky is the type to settle for just any man.'

'She'll find out eventually what type of man you are, Wynn.'

Wynn turned his head and rode silently ahead in silence. Dave maintained his silence. Wynn kept his thoughts to himself. He wanted to turn around and go back to the house, throw his arms around Becky, and ask her to be his woman.

Rodeo and Nick McCallum had been riding on in grim, heavy silence. Nick was swaying in the saddle. Their conversation was of a different sort.

'Just keep me on my horse until we get there, Rodeo.'

'I promise,' he answered. Then fell

into a glum mood, weaving his through the ground fog, which had begun to settle again.

'What's wrong, Rodeo?'

'Well, for one thing we've got two herds of horses we have to get down to Collier before the big snows begin, and we've got three men to work with.'

'It's been done before now.'

'Has it? Maybe with cattle, but we're going to be griping and cussing the whole way.'

'We've got that Dave, now. He looks like a healthy enough specimen to me.'

'Maybe,' Rodeo pondered, 'but who says he's riding for Collier or that he'd be willing to work with us.'

'Why not? He has to go through Collier anyway if he's heading home to Cheyenne.'

'We could at least ask him,' Rodeo figured. 'I put that stage loot where I told you. It'll still be there if the town don't burn down in the meantime.'

'Yeah, I know you did. That didn't really go all that bad. Why did that town man have a thirty-caliber rifle with him?'

'It's just the way our luck played out. No sense in complaining about it now.'

'I'm not complaining,' Nick said. 'I bought my ticket to the fair. It's just that it hurts so bad, Rodeo. Can't you remember the last time you were bad hurt?'

'Yeah, I remember — you thought that it was funny to tickle my feet with chicken feathers.'

Nick either could not think of something to say in return, or the constant pain was eating through him. After a while he did say, 'I believe I'll go on over and talk to Dave and Wynn . . . about the trail plans and all.'

'Sit where you are, Nick, you're doing fine. I want you at least to be in the saddle when we reach the ranch.'

'Are you saying I won't be good for much anything else?' Nick asked peevishly.

Rodeo shook his head silently. He had said all he had to say. Besides, as they crested the last flat hummock in front of the Porter ranch and came before the house, Rodeo began to wonder if they weren't on a fool's mission. A badly wounded man, a man who wore a star, and two McCallum boys.

And below them, neatly lined along the hitch rail, were six fog-streaked saddle horses.

The two brothers held up their own ponies to wait for Dave Chandler and Wynn to draw alongside.

'What is it?' Dave asked in a whisper.

'This — you said there were three of the Guilefords down there. I believe we have six horses showing and there could be more in the barn.

'It looks like it,' Dave answered. Moisture was gathering on their hats and trickling past their eyes. The wind from the north was slanting in just enough to be uncomfortable. 'Are you going to go home, Rodeo?'

'Hell, no, I ain't going home! What do you think I am? People think I'm a rash man, that I move about at random.

But I like to know everything I can about a situation, and this one was represented to me to be a little different than I find.'

Nick's voice was a low growl. 'Let's get on down there, Rodeo. Personally I don't care how many they are. They're bothering our neighbors, challenging us. If the captain were still with us, he'd be charging that cabin right now instead of talking it over.'

'Look, Nick,' Rodeo argued, 'I know you don't much care what happens . . . '

' . . . because I'm going to die here, anyway,' Nick said, his temper flaring up a little.

Rodeo's face grew wooden again. 'Maybe you are, maybe you aren't, but you can't go slinging lead around the Duchess's parlor.'

The front door to the Porter house opened, letting a square wedge of firelight slip from the cozy interior of the house. Behind that light Dave could see men moving across the floor, the shadowed face of Tammany, and another whom he thought was Gent Guileford. The door shut again before he could even guess at who the others were.

'Has someone got an idea of how we can get Rose Ann out of the house before we go down after them?'

'Yeah,' Rodeo said, 'I do, if a man has the nerve for it.'

Rodeo picked his man and after a few minutes conference, Dave Chandler started down the slope toward the house. Were there Guileford men in the barn? How many? Maybe they should have rigged another pony for the old lady, but no one had wanted to take the time to do it.

Besides, Dave had to admit darkly, there was every chance that the task he had taken up was simply impossible and that he and the Duchess would be dead before the sun went down. He tugged down his fog-slick hat, looked toward the reddish glow that was the Porter house's hearth light and slogged forward aboard his weary piebald.

8

He was still out there. At first as the day dimmed and grew cooler, Becky Porter had thought that the sounds were of wild animals foraging around, but they were not. She sat on a wooden chair at the table of the fortress-like McCallum house, an old Army pistol dangling from her hands. It hadn't been hard to find a weapon in this house. She could hardly look anywhere without seeing one. Pistols were on tables, on ledges, under the furniture — and the telling things was that every one of these was oiled and loaded.

Becky shifted in her chair. She kept her movements small. No one had to tell her that she had landed herself in a bad situation here. She had assumed as had everyone else that if Darby Guileford had followed them, he would have gone away after seeing the

McCallums arrive home. He hadn't.

He was out there now, prowling in the dark. Darby wasn't very bright, perhaps, but once he had the scent of a woman, he was bound to keep on her trail.

Something crashed in the barn. There was a terrific racket as if a stack of milk cans had fallen. Nervously, Becky snatched at the old Colt, nearly dropping it to the floor.

The keening winds swatted at the house, producing small moans and eerie whistles. The firelight wavered as the wind tagged at it down the chimney.

She should have accepted the offer to leave Dave Chandler with her, but she knew he hadn't really wanted to stay. There was going to be a battle at her own house and she knew that each of the men figured to take a hand in it. They needed all the men they had, and they could have used more. Where was Kit McCallum?

Had she remained behind hoping to see him alone? Why? What was there to say that she hadn't already said? Kit was a reckless man, she knew. At times she wondered how she would ever be able to tame the wild young cowboy. A heavy crash came from the roof above Becky.

Someone was up there, though; she could hear boots slowly proceeding across the flat roof. There was no doubt as to who it was. There could only be one white man within miles that she knew of. And, a man who meant no mischief would have presented himself at the front door.

There was no sense in pretending — it was the blank-eyed Darby Guileford up there, trying to find a way into the house. Perhaps he had seen Wynn up there earlier, and reasoned there had to be a way down.

Well, of course there had to be, Becky realized. She had to find it before Darby did. Starting across the room, the blood pounding at her temples, the Colt clenched tightly in her hand, she came upon the free-standing ladder which was used to reach a trap door above. As she looked up, the square of timber suddenly vibrated in its nook. A thin trickle of dirt fell into the room as the door was yanked open to reveal the night sky above. And then the entrance above was filled with a leering, unbalanced face. A single arm reached down toward her and Becky stepped away. She thumbed at the hammer of the ancient Colt, drew it back, and she stammered, 'D-don't move — I'll — I'll shoot! I'm warning you — I'll do it!' But her words seemed to only amuse the single-minded Darby Guileford.

A sound at the front door made Becky think rescue had come and she started that way in relief. Darby took that moment to launch himself into the room, both arms raised, his mouth open in a silent grimace. He reached for her, grabbing the corner of her blouse. She jerked away wildly, tripped over a discarded boot on the floor, and the gun fired upward.

The force of the old pistol in her hands as it spewed fire rocked her back on her heels. The gun fired again. An inhuman shriek filled her ears. Darby's arms wind-milled; he slapped at his face, momentarily hiding behind his hands, and when he pulled them away, she saw what she had done.

The side of his face was gone, from the outer orbit of his eye on back. He had paid a savage price for his lust. Darby Guileford collapsed onto the wooden floor with a heavy thud. He landed with the macabre remainder of his face up. And Becky turned away, about to be sick. She could smell him; he needed a bath.

As the echo of the shot slowly faded and the black smoke dissipated, she became once again aware of the pounding on the front door.

'Open this door! What's going on in there?'

In a daze, Becky stumbled that way, fumbled with the latch, and swung the door in . . . to find Kit McCallum standing there in the gloom of evening, pistol in hand, wearing both a look of concern and a boyish grin.

'Who fired a gun off in here?'

He noticed the inert body of Darby Guileford on the floor beyond Becky then and asked, 'Who's that? Who shot him? How'd he get in?' Becky was left with little time to respond. Kit nudged his way past her and walked to the body, dripping moisture as he went.

As Kit crouched down over the body, Becky told him, 'He came in through the roof. No one was up there to watch.' That comment intended to shame Kit had no such effect.

'I'll just be a minute, Becky,' Kit said. From outside someone was yelling through the fog and drizzle.

Straining, Becky could hear a woman's voice shouting, 'Hurry up! I don't want to be sitting too long out here!'

Kit returned his gun to its holster and now smiling, began digging through his clothing shelves. 'I just need my winter coat and a few shirts. You can tell Rodeo . . . oh, hell, I don't think there's anything you can tell him except that I'm traveling on down the road.'

Becky could not think to ask any questions or get replies to them. She was still trembling from what she had just done. She sat down numbly on the couch again, and watched Kit's back as he threw his few clothes into a flour sack, slipped into his winter coat, and was away again.

'Goodbye, Becky,' he called with a wink and a smile as he returned to the door.

'Kit!' Becky cried out and he turned to look at her. She found that she could not say what she had had in mind. She only asked, 'Will you drag this man outside for me?'

That was all there was to their final meeting. Becky managed to make her way to the front window and she watched as Kit McCallum turned his horse away from the ranch house accompanied by a small woman with very long black hair.

Becky watched them go until the distance and the fog swallowed them up. Then she returned to the couch and sat staring at the flickering firelight through her tears as the fog drew heavier yet and closed around the stone house.

★   ★   ★

'You know what you're supposed to do?' Rodeo McCallum asked Dave Chandler, not for the first time.

'Yeah, I do,' Dave said a little irritably. 'I only hope it works.'

'That all depends on you, doesn't it?' Rodeo said, still surveying the Porter house where hopeful smoke rose from the stone chimney into the clotted sky.

'I suppose so,' Dave answered with a heavy sigh.

'If we're going to do something, let's get to it! I'd like to be here to see the end of it.' This was Nick McCallum, who belonged home in bed or in a grave. He sat his horse fairly well, but he was wobbling. His face was parchment yellow, his body still leaking blood and quivering. His eyes were like fire agates in the night.

Dave started his piebald around toward the back of the house. The night was still, the air misting and heavy. He wiped the moisture from his eyes and continued on, angled toward the back kitchen porch. The damp ground muffled the sounds of his horse's hoofs. Through the yellow window blind he could see a man standing in the corner, smoking a pipe, no one else. Then there was a brief bustling movement and the inner door opened to allow Rose Ann to pass into the kitchen with a tray full of empty plates.

Dave waited for the clattering of dishes into the wash tub to subside, then he steeled himself and stepped out of leather and up to the back door. He knocked on the door only to avoid being shot out of hand and then opened it and stepped in, half expecting a slug of hot lead to interrupt his journey.

The man with the pipe had drawn his pistol and stepped back, but the outlaw whose name was Arnold Tyler was a new arrival and did not know what was what on the Porter ranch; he wasn't going to go about popping off strangers. He had been enjoying his visit to the warm kitchen, talking on and off with the genial Rose Ann Porter. It reminded him of the days he had enjoyed in his grandmother's kitchen before he had 'gone bad'.

Rose Ann spun from the sink, her eyes asking questions. 'Dave, what is it? What's happened?'

'It's Becky,' Dave told her. 'She's taken a tumble over at the McCallum place. We're afraid to move her. She wants you.'

'Oh my goodness,' the Duchess said as she whipped off her apron, glanced toward the inner door, and was hurried out into the night by Dave Chandler.

Arnold Tyler could only frown and watch them go. He had no instructions on how to handle such a situation, but in fact he had not been posted as a guard. He scratched his head and took another kitchen match to re-light his pipe.

Reaching his horse, Dave said, 'Get up!' in a tone he would never have used to address the Duchess at any other time.

'I take it Becky is all right?' Rose Ann said as Dave mounted behind her and started the piebald back for the shelter of the woods.

'She is, or at least she was the last time I saw her, sitting in front of the fireplace in the McCallum house.'

The old woman was wise to much. 'I take it Rodeo has taken a hand?' she asked as the piebald walked on. There was no need to run the poor beast.

'He has.'

'I figured it was something like that. Rodeo McCallum is too well known to have shown his own face.'

'Is he?' Dave asked idly. He himself had not known the McCallums before the past few days, but perhaps Rodeo and the others were known to be bad men up here — there certainly had been a few indications that the McCallums were interested in occupations other than ranching, but Dave had no warrants on them and you can't go around arresting men on suspicion alone.

In minutes they had reached the camp where the others waited. Wynn McCallum was the first to the horse to help the Duchess down. Rodeo fixed his dark eyes on Dave and nodded his satisfaction.

'Let's go or I'm taking it on myself to do it,' Nick said through his pain and fury.

'We go,' Rodeo said soberly. He swung into the saddle. Dave started to follow, but Rodeo told him, 'You stay with the Duchess, lawman, just let us take care of cleaning out this rats' nest.'

Again? Last time Rodeo had tried to leave him behind with Becky, now he was to baby sit the Duchess. Either Rodeo didn't trust Dave's shooting or he didn't trust the marshal to know his targets. Either way, it was obvious that

Rodeo didn't want Dave around him with a gun, and so he stood beside the Duchess, watching as the three McCallum boys disappeared through the gloom.

'Those boys are just the best neighbors an old woman could have,' the Duchess said to Dave. 'But tell me, what's wrong with Nick?'

'They're saying his horse threw him,' Dave replied.

'Oh no! That fine roan of his? When you saw them riding by it was as if they were one glorious animal.'

'Yes, ma'am. I don't know what happened they said the horse stepped in a prairie dog hole.'

Dave studied the doughty old woman closely. Her jaw was set but managed to carry a smile as she looked out toward the house where all remained momentarily silent. Her back was straight, her shoulders held squarely. Her eyes were steady, accepting of whatever was to come. He wondered what she had been like as a young woman. He could understand why the McCallum boys were loyal to her.

'Rose Ann, I have to ask you a favor.'

She turned quick eyes to him. 'Yes?' she said.

'Will you take that black-and-white horse of mine and ride to the McCallum place? This business that's about to happen concerns me as much as anyone. You probably know that I am a lawman . . . ?'

'I saw your badge on the first night you were here.'

Dave smiled; of course she would have seen it. 'I've got to be in on what's happening, Rose Ann. The territory wants the Guilefords brought in for a robbery and murder they've done.'

'Then you don't want to arrest those nice McCallum boys.'

'No, ma'am, I have nothing on them.'

'Well, people do talk, you know,' she said. 'I've heard malicious things said about the McCallums. But if it's the Guilefords you're after, Marshal, grab for your patch and grab for your rod!'

Dave needed no such gear, just a little extra willingness to enter the line of fire. The sound of the first shot from near the house below provided that, and he handed the piebald over to the Duchess.

'Kit might be at home now, I don't know. But you and Becky will be safe in that old stone fort the McCallums have built,' he said, helping her aboard his horse.

Another shot had sounded and a third. 'How will you get home?' the Duchess asked worriedly, and that was an easy question to answer.

'I've a feeling there's going to be more than one extra horse to ride after this is over,' he shouted. Then he slapped the piebald's flank and sent it loping toward the west, the Duchess erect on its back.

Then Dave, carrying his Winchester rifle at the ready, began a slow, steady run down the slope of the hill to the house where hellfire had risen to stitch across the silence of the weary night.

9

Something was stuffing up the chimney above the fireplace in the Porter house. Smoke was backing up badly toward the doors and windows. Dave only hoped the building was not on fire. He reckoned the McCallum boys would spend months rebuilding the house for the women if need be. And they would come ready to do the job.

He had a thought that he would remain around to help them if that were the case.

Dave ran forward, staggering, stumbling down the damp hill toward the smoking Porter house. He could see now that the McCallum boys had gone directly toward the house under Rodeo's directions. Silhouettes of the men appeared before the house, darting across the yard as firearms within blazed away at their half-seen attackers.

Someone within had picked out Dave Chandler from the shadows, for two rifle shots were fired in quick progression at him as he stormed down through the fog from the hill slope. One bullet passed so near to his face that he could feel its breeze fanning his eyelashes. Another punched into the damp earth not far from his boot heel. The man below had his range.

Dave flung himself forward. Kissing the damp grass, he saw a banshee on a gray horse burst from the barn. Dave had dropped his Winchester in his fall, now he struggled to snag his Colt from its holster as the horseman charged down on him. The rider wore an unbuttoned military coat and was hatless. At first sight he knew the man to be Tammany Guileford himself, deserting the body of his men, using their shots for cover. Dave fired awkwardly at the fleeing man. His first shot missed Tammany completely. His second, fired in anger, seemed to tag the gray horse in the left rear fetlock, passing clean through.

Someone screamed from inside the house. The front door was thrown open and a man emerged, his hair on fire, the Colt in his hand bucking. He was enraged, fighting savagely against his own death, but he would not win.

Dave watched the man die — not from the fire but from a bullet hidden deep within his body at some critical point. It was obvious that the McCallums were outmanned; it was also obvious to the Guilefords that though they might be accomplished thieves, their fighting skills were not up to those of the terrible McCallums. Dave watched Nick McCallum at the threshold of the front door with two Colt revolvers blazing, as the Guileford boys peeled away in panic.

There was nothing to stop Nick. He was already dead on his feet. Dave watched four, five bullets punch through his body as he assaulted them, throwing him this way and that. But his hands were alive and the hammers of those Colts continued to function, to ratchet back and fall again spewing retribution into the bodies of the men who had come there to harm his mother. Nick's legs wobbled and he sank to the floor in the smoky confusion of the house.

Dave glanced once in the direction Tammany had ridden astride his injured gray horse, but he knew he couldn't run down even a crippled horse afoot, and so he turned his attention back to the Porter house. Finding his rifle on the damp grass, he snatched it up and shambled on again. Circling toward the back of a house he saw a waiting silhouette behind a boxy, untended oak tree. He knew the man by his clothes.

'Rodeo,' he said in a low voice as a dozen more shots were snapped off in the front yard behind him. 'It's Dave.'

'All right. Come ahead. I was about ready to shoot you. Where's the Duchess?'

'I sent her along to your house on my horse.'

Rodeo made an approving grunted sound. 'Did you see Wynn out front?'

'No, just Nick. He did his best, but he's out of the fight now.'

'Wait!' Rodeo held up a hand. 'Did you hear that — that's Wynn shooting.'

'How can you tell?'

'I've lived with the man for over twenty years, that's how. Wynn always will fire two shots in a row once he's tagged his man. He wants to make sure the man is hit hard. It would seem a waste of ammunition, but I can see Wynn's way of thinking too. My dad couldn't break him of the habit and I figured I'm not going to either. That's Wynn. So he's at the north end of the house. Those Guileford boys must figure we've got them trapped in the house. Not one's even tried for their horses.'

'Tammany broke out,' Dave informed him. 'They must have thought he was going for their horses, but he just took his and rode out hard for the west.'

'Toward our place!' Rodeo displayed his anger.

'I don't know how well he knows this

country. I had the feeling he was riding just to be going away.'

'Better be. Who's left at the ranch?'

A flurry of shots broke off their conversation; bark was ripped from the oak by a trio of bullets. Rodeo McCallum stood tall in silhouette against the occasional moon. His Stetson cut a distinct, sharp outline. His face was every bit as angular, and it was set hard as he figured out their odds. Rodeo would not back down; Dave knew that. The skirmish had already cost him a brother.

With the guns in the house momentarily silent, Dave answered Rodeo. 'Kit might have come back to the house by now. We know Becky is there, and Rose Ann should be arriving soon.'

'Of the three I'd most trust the Duchess to hold the fort,' Rodeo muttered. Then, tired of talking and fruitless planning, he tugged his hat down another inch and said, 'Well, mister lawman, let's get this house cleaned out for the ladies.'

Coming up at the corner of the house

where they could not be seen out any window, they held up and Rodeo yelled out something in Spanish that Dave didn't get. From the other end of the house, Wynn McCallum answered, also in Spanish.

'Did you understand?' Rodeo asked. Dave Chandler just shook his head.

'It's just another thing my father brought up from Texas with him. None of us speaks it well or has much use for it — except maybe Kit — but from time to time we don't want others knowin' what we know.'

'What are we going to do?' Dave asked.

'There's another window just like this one on that end of the house,' Rodeo told him. 'We're both going to take a window and open up. You have any idea how hard it is to stay away from all the windows in a house? Especially for a group of men. Usually it's the last thing they've thought of.'

'You're just going to gun them down?' Dave asked. It wasn't the way he had learned his peacekeeping.

'What did you think they were going to do with us in the end?' Rodeo asked sharply. He slipped fresh brass cartridges into his guns. Then he stepped to the window which faced the Duchess's bedroom, cracked the glass with the muzzle of his Colt, and got to firing.

From the north end of the house answering fire chattered. Now, having learned the trick, Dave could identify the shots as Wynn McCallum's. Dave couldn't stand there like a dummy. Not liking Rodeo's style of fighting, he decided to ease up to the corner once again and try to stop anyone who would be trying to exit the house the back way in a hurry.

Those inside the house would not know how many assailants were outside; their only thought would be to escape, and any man or animal knowing that danger lay in one direction would naturally try to flee the opposite way.

The spring door opened as Dave reached it and then the solid rear kitchen door. Three men tried to exit the house at once, and they were right in Dave's sights as they spilled outside. Some ingrained training caused Dave Chandler to shout out, 'Hold it! This is the law!'

It was futile. All of these gathered men were living a life which caused them to drift them from one crime to the other, the hangman at their heels. They had to fight back. They turned as one in a tangled mass, guns at the ready.

They had no chance.

Coming from light to darkness they could not definitely identify Dave in the uncertain, fog-patched night. But he was able to pick out their confused, shocked faces. Gent Guileford sent out a wild shot at Dave, which was too close for his liking.

Dave wasted no time in answering the Guilefords. He did have the advantage, and despite what Rodeo might have gathered from his demeanor, this was hardly Dave Chandler's first gunfight. And the boys down south carried weapons as well.

From the far end of the house a Stetson perched on the muzzle of a Winchester rifle poked out tentatively from behind the planks.

'Come on ahead, Wynn!' Dave called out, for Dave had heard the many guns firing at the rear of the house followed by a prolonged silence. He knew that men had died, he just couldn't tell in the darkness who it had been.

'That you, Dave?' Wynn McCallum yelled back.

'It's me.'

'Where's Rodeo?'

'I'm right here,' Rodeo answered. 'First things first, boys — let's make sure they're all cleared out of the house.'

Dave circled the house and entered by the front door while Rodeo and Wynn cleared off the kitchen porch and went in that way. Stepping over the dead, Rodeo hooted once to let Dave Chandler know that they were now in the house. A little caution can save a tragic mistake when nerves were running so high.

Dave came upon Nick's body first thing. He hadn't even known the man, but Nick had proven himself a tough article and he had gone out fighting for two women who were unable to do it for themselves. He looked around with care. The two men on the floor directly in front of Nick McCallum had undoubtedly fallen to his blazing Colts. A third man not far beyond these in the bare wood hallway had taken a bullet from the window on the end.

'All right to come through?' Rodeo called from the kitchen.

'It's all quiet in here. Someone should look in the women's closets in case some fool was crazy enough to try hiding in there.'

Rodeo strode away into the Duchess's bedroom while Wynn emerged into the front room which had scattered brass strewn everywhere. Wynn stopped, standing over Nick's twisted body.

'He should never have tried to come,'

Wynn said sorrowfully. 'Nick was already just about dead before we got here.'

Rodeo glanced toward his brother but did not stop on his way to the other bedroom which was Becky's.

'Don't like going into a lady's bedroom,' Rodeo said on his return. It seemed an odd comment for this hard-bitten man, but we all have our standards.

Dave reloaded his handgun. It was during this process that he noticed the blood leaking down his own pant leg. He could not remember being hit, but he obviously had been. Now that he was aware of it, a dull ache began throbbing in his calf, and he hobbled to the couch to sit there.

Rodeo said to his brother, 'We've got to get this place cleaned up a little, Wynn. Go to the barn and see about getting the wagon, if there's any animals who are fit to pull it. If you spot any shovels fit for grave digging, toss them in the wagon bed for us. We'll have use for them tonight. We'll clean it up as best we can for the Duchess and Becky.'

'I can sweep up the brass and the widow glass,' Dave volunteered. But as he tried to rise from the leather couch, he could feel his leg already seizing up on him. For a moment he thought he was going to fall.

Watching the display, Rodeo said, 'You'll be no help here. It pains me to think of you trying to dig a grave. Go along, lawman, maybe you can help them out at the stone house. I'd feel better knowing they had another gun around the place. There's no telling what Kit is doing.'

'All right,' Dave agreed, 'it will give me the chance to find out where Tammany Guileford has gotten to. There's a clearing moon; I should be able to track him by it, being he's the only man who could have passed that way.' He paused then added, 'I need a horse.'

Rodeo was quick to reply. 'Take the one Nick was riding. He won't be needing it any more. You know enough to tell anybody that asks that you got it back from a gang of horse thieves, don't you?'

'I guess I do,' Marshal Chandler said, eyeing Rodeo McCallum closely. Rodeo still seemed to have a low opinion of Dave. In truth Dave had no idea where the horse Nick McCallum had been riding had come from. It didn't matter. Most of the horses he would be able to catch up on that night were likely stolen ones.

Just now, he had to trust Rodeo McCallum. He had to rely on the men who had fought with him. He couldn't call them friends, but he knew the McCallum brothers, for the time being, at least, were on his side, and that was strangely comforting.

10

The fog was settled in patches across the broad Wyoming plains. Low, sometimes heavy clouds of spun dampness would clot the hollows, hide the forest approaches, and then part before the full moon at unpredictable intervals to reveal a fairyland of shadowed trees and the long vista.

Dave had already spotted the tracks of the gray horse Tammany Guileford was riding. They lined out straight if not swiftly toward the area of the McCallum ranch house. It seemed to Dave that Guileford was riding directly west in the direction of the rugged coulee that the Duchess had described to him when he had first arrived. It was said there was no crossing this scar in the earth if your name was not McCallum.

Dave Chandler was hoping he

wouldn't have to find out if this was a fact. If Guileford had started toward the button hook portion of the trail, it indicated that he knew the coulee's path that well. It did not mean he knew how to make it across, and he wasn't going to be riding much longer, not on the injured gray. The horse was obviously dragging its left rear leg now. Maybe Guileford's whole intent was to make the McCallum house and borrow yet another horse — after all, he knew where the McCallum brothers were at this moment, and he might have figured he had little to fear from them.

It was still Dave Chandler's job to find the man and bring him in if he could. It was the Guilefords who had robbed the bank in Medicine Bow and committed murder in the process.

It had to have been — though Dave had no proof, for there could be none — the Guilefords who had killed the smiling, bespectacled Virgil Dodd, who against all advice had decided to come tracking the bank robbers on his own.

He had found them, it seemed, over at Rambler Shack.

Because of that, it mattered a lot to Dave to run down Tammany, if it could be done. He carried arrest warrants for the three known Guilefords: Tammany, Gent and Darby. Gent, he did know, was now waiting while his grave was prepared on the Porter ranch. Dave had shot Gent himself. He did not know where Darby was. That question could wait until later to be answered. In the meantime, he had his sights set on Tammany, and meant to keep them focused there. A lone, loveless bird cast a sudden dark shadow against the face of the full moon. Dave flicked a short glance that way, patted the horse's neck, and rode grimly forward through the fog and silence of the night.

The tracks left by Tammany Guileford showed that when he reached the button hook byway, he followed it, avoiding the trench nature had carved into the earth. He had probably gotten his information from the Duchess, perhaps sitting at her kitchen table to draw map as she had for Dave. Tammany knew where he was going and Dave thought he knew why. The horse the man rode was now hobbling badly, limping its pained way along.

Tammany Guileford knew full well that the McCallums had horses, and plenty of them now that they had made their gather. An already-broken saddle mount could be found at the ranch itself — if Tammany could make it that far on his crippled horse.

A bobcat broke from the trees, hissed once at Dave, and started again on its way. Anyone who had only seen them in magazines thought them to be cute little cats with tufted ears. But anyone who had seen one loose in a chicken coop or tearing up a yard dog knew they were forty pounds of terror.

The oaks were thick again and scattered pines filled the gaps and as Dave rode his horse through the trees, he slowed a little and took his Colt revolver into his hand once again. There were many tangled shadows deceiving the senses. An owl dove low at his head, decided Dave was too large to carry away and glided on.

He could smell wood smoke now, which didn't seem right as the stone house was still far distant. But the night was still and his senses on high alert.

Where had Tammany gotten to? He should have come upon him by now. His leg had stopped throbbing, and instead begun to burn with the fire of a deep puncture wound. Dave had the idea that the bullet had gone completely through his calf, but had never taken the time to examine it. It was childish, of course, but one just didn't drop his trousers in front of Rodeo McCallum.

Rodeo wasn't hard to figure out. There were hundreds of men like him in the western lands. He was trying to live out Steamboat Bill's dream for him as best he could, with the tools he had been given as a boy. When Bill had died, Rodeo had three orphaned younger brothers to consider. It would have been a tough life, and he had grown tough —

The gunshot like a clap of thunder out of a cloudless sky startled Dave Chandler as well as the bay horse, which had been half asleep while it plodded along, not knowing where it was going or why or when it would get there. The sudden shot made them both fully alert.

Dave ducked automatically, pointlessly, and brought his pistol up as the bay kicked out in a way that Dave knew from experience meant that the horse was ready to run — anywhere.

Dave tight-fisted the reins and calmed the horse, which he had nearly accomplished before a second shot rang out and its following echo rolled across the land. Dave looked in every direction, searching for anything — a night figure, drifting smoke, a hunting night animal, but he saw nothing beyond the trees where he had been riding, heard nothing more.

Dave tried to get his bearings in this

unfamiliar land. He was near to the place where the trees thinned and then fell away, forming the level stretch that led to the northern yard which abutted the McCallum's stone house. He thought he heard the whicker of a horse, probably one of those captured and penned in the pole corral farther to the west.

He looked around again, hoping almost frantically for help to arrive. The sturdy, familiar faces of Rodeo and Wynn would be fine to see just now, even though he knew they could not have had the time to finish what they were doing.

It was his leg wound, he decided, that was causing him to feel that way. His body needed help and rest and it knew it. Lost, alone, and wounded in a cold night in strange country with someone out there shooting: it was not an enviable situation to find himself in.

Slowly approaching the forest verge once more, he found that he had guessed where he was correctly. He had emerged near here on his first approach to the McCallum house with Becky. Thinking of Becky, he wondered what had become of the half-wit brother of Tammany Guileford.

A few hundred yards on aboard the slow-gaited bay horse, Dave Chandler had nearly convinced himself that he was worrying over nothing. Darby had likely gone wandering on his way like some lost hound. Why did he believe that? Because the stone house was virtually impregnable and had been designed that way. The two earlier shots might have been a brief, deadly exchange of an attacker against those holding the house. Kit McCallum might well have returned to the house by now and startled Guileford trying to slip up without being seen.

Any such visitor would have met the angry resistance of Kit and his Colt .44.

That was all conjecture, and Dave did not like guessing games. After a dip into a shallow grassy swale and a climb back out on the tough little bay. Dave saw something which made matters clearer — and also confused them.

The gray horse lay sprawled against the moon-silvered grass, the dark stain of blood smeared against its skull. Tammany Guileford had put the wounded animal down with a shot behind the ear.

Then why the second shot?

Could someone else nearby been startled by Tammany's shot and automatically fired back? Perhaps the missing Darby, shooting blindly at his own brother in the night? There was no telling, and Dave was getting tired of guessing at things he might never know. The only things that were certain were that Tammany had put his horse down and was now within walking distance of a place where plenty of fresh horses were sheltered — the McCallum ranch. Dave hoped that Kit had come home and been alerted by the shots and that he and the youngest McCallum brother now had the bank robber caught between them.

* ★ *

'I saw the man that time for sure, Becky,' the Duchess said as she stood with a Winchester in her hands, peering out one of the northern slit windows of the stone McCallum house. 'Couldn't miss him in that moonlight.'

'I couldn't stand it if another one made his way inside,' Becky said, still unnerved over having to shoot Darby Guileford after his rude entrance through the roof of the house.

'You don't have a thing to worry about, girl. Not so long as I'm here, but,' she added in a mutter, 'I do wish we had one of those McCallum boys with us.'

They had had one, Becky thought — Kit McCallum — but he had not cared enough about her welfare to delay his flight with Alicia. Becky had learned the Spanish girl's name some time back. She held no more than a slight grudge against Alicia; it was not her fault that Kit preferred what Alicia had to share over her own poor offerings.

Becky, too, could not help but wish that somehow the McCallum boys would return. From what Rose Ann said they had been preparing for battle with the Guilefords when her aunt left. They could have all been killed by now for all the women knew. Nick had not looked well when they rode out toward the Porter ranch.

It would have been so fine to see the implacable Rodeo McCallum come riding in on his big pinto horse. It was impossible to think of Rodeo ever being bested in a gun fight. And Wynn, so loyal and faithful, always doing his best to be closer to Becky, a hard man with a large streak of kindness . . .

Rose Ann Porter's rifle racketed at the window as she squeezed off a shot. Without turning her head, he said, 'I think I got him that time. I must have. He went down hard.'

★   ★   ★

Dave Chandler saw the rifle explode from the narrow window of the stone house, saw the man in black trying to cross the grassy yard go down and remain there. Dismounting from the somewhat skittish bay he was riding he approached the still figure on foot, not knowing if he would find a man lying in wait or the figure of Tammany Guileford sprawled dead upon the dewy grass.

There was no telling; Dave had seen the man go down hard following the rifle shot, but he may have been only playing possum. At least he knew that someone in the house had weapons and knew how to use them. It figured to be Kit McCallum, for if he had returned and found only Becky there, alone, he was sure to stick with her for protection, wasn't he?

With his own well-being in mind, Dave hollered out toward the house, 'It's Dave Chandler here; don't fire at me!'

He covered the remaining dozen

paces with one eye on the house, the other on the downed man. The moonlight was brighter than ever, yet Dave saw no glint from the fallen man's eyes.

He took another step, and as he did Tammany Guileford rose from the ground like a big cat, growled, and closed the distance between himself and Dave, driving his shoulder into the marshal's chest as Dave raised his pistol, firing, and missing at his adversary. From the window of the house came more rifle fire, two rapid shots, one of which struck metal and sang off into the night. Another struck flesh. Tammany spun back and away, his own pistol touched off in the process sending a hot projectile at Dave Chandler, driving him to the cold moonlit yard.

11

Dave Chandler was hit again. A hard-hitting .44 slug had bored its way through his right thigh. He had approached Tammany Guileford's body with his pistol drawn, moving cautiously toward the bad man. But not quite carefully enough. Guileford was a wily old catamount who had been trapped, shot out, and taken down before. None of this was enough to make him quit. The shot from Tammany's Colt flooded the marshal with the instant pain and shock of the impact.

Guileford was on his feet again instantly. He ran past Dave, grabbing for the reins of the lawman's bay, but he missed and had to run on as another close rifle shot boomed from the stone house. The bay bolted. Guileford ran on, staggering now. Dave Chandler, glancing once after his lost, panicked horse, tried to pursue on foot. It was futile. With one leg burning with pain, the other throbbing, his head pounding with each beat, his inelegant progress must have made him a pitiable sight.

He did not know where Tammany Guileford had gotten to. The only thing that made any sense was the old stone barn where the McCallum boys kept their spare riding stock.

Guileford would be in a hurry for a horse and he would need one that was rested and quick — which McCallum Big M mounts would be.

Dave started that way, caught a familiar form from the corner of his eye: his own big black and white piebald on which he had sent the Duchess here was standing in front of the house, listless head bowed, looking tired, bored, and uncertain at once. He made an immediate choice — while Guileford was fumbling in the dark for a horse, saddle, and bridle — there stood the big piebald, already outfitted and known to Dave.

He checked the saddle cinches to

make sure Rose Ann had left them tight, which she had in her rush to get inside, and with exquisite pain forced his left boot up to the stirrup and swung his stiff right leg over the piebald's back. Surrounding the drooping reins with his fingers, Dave turned the horse, adjusting his position to ease his legs as best he could.

Simultaneously the barn door was opened and Tammany Guileford, silhouetted before a dim lantern, appeared there on a lanky red horse, saw Dave, and slapped his heels to the horse he rode, starting it forward at a brisk pace.

Gritting his teeth, Dave turned the piebald's head and started after Guileford. As much as they both have wished for it, their night was not over yet. Dave rode through the settling darkness at an uncomfortable pace. The door to the stone house briefly opened behind him and he heard the Duchess's voice ring out to follow him as he cleared the yard: 'Atta boy, Dave! Ride the polecat down!'

165

That was much easier said than done. As the two riders pounded away toward the west, in the direction of the coulee, Dave was losing ground with each minute. The piebald was eager enough, but it never been that supple. Dave preferred it as a long-riding horse, not as a quarter-miler. The red horse, on the other hand, was younger, fresher, more limber: a true racer, which was probably why Tammany Guileford had grabbed it up.

The young horse undoubtedly had the speed to outrace the piebald to Collier town, and once there Guileford could trade horses again and be well on his way, leaving Deputy Marshal Dave Chandler far in his dust.

Dave felt like whipping the piebald, slapping spurs to it, but that would have been pointless; the big horse could only run as fast as it could, and Dave was already getting that from it.

He followed Tammany through a wind break of young poplars and emerged again on the moonlit prairie.

Directly ahead now a broad shadow crossed the earth, a time- and water-cut gorge, which Tammany had either forgotten about or recklessly believed he could cross. The coulee wended its way generally southward through a jumbled tangle of trees and boulders, its banks as much as fifty-feet deep composed of nothing but sand and crumbling red rock. Once down in it . . .

What had the Duchess said? 'If your name's not McCallum, you'll never find a way across it.'

Even as Dave was thinking of that he caught sight of the lost, enraged, pain-stricken outlaw forcing his stolen horse forward over the lip of the coulee, perhaps thinking he had seen a path down and a way up and out on the farther slope by moonlight.

Perhaps he had. The cagey old Steamboat Bill had built his ranch to be virtually impregnable, but there always had to be a way in for the Texas man and his sons, did there not?

Dave was left with no good choices. He thought he could probably ride along the western bluff, following Tammany, who would have to slow for the heavy brush and rock falls in the coulee bottom. But the marshal did not even know if the chasm forked at some point, one canyon meeting another.

He could find himself left impossibly far behind then.

Following Tammany blindly into the gorge could find Dave lost as well, an easy prey for a waiting rifleman as he made his way, clomping blindly ahead.

'Well?' he asked the piebald. He thought the horse seemed less inclined to follow the outlaw down into the coulee. 'Let's follow along up here for a while. That fine young pony of his is bound to get tired after crossing rock-jumbles, drifted logs, and clumps of dead brush.

'I don't think he can make it up the far side; from what I see, it's unlikely. If he does, I'll just have to admit he's beaten me and wait for another day to finish matters with Tammany Guileford.'

The piebald horse made no answer.

Dave's wounds were starting to throb badly. His right leg ached with fiery pain and was leaking hot blood again.

He had a sudden vision of himself, brave plains marshal, being found as a coyote-gnawed pile of bones in the remote Wyoming badlands. He was, he realized, growing light-headed and allowing his mind to drift away from what should have been keeping him fully alert — the pursuit of the outlaw Tammany Guileford.

Riding close to the crumbling edge of the coulee, he had a clear view down into its depths where the lone man was trying desperately to find his way out and make his escape. Dave could have reached out and shot the man with his handgun, and if things became impossible, he decided, he would do just that. But Tammany had trapped himself like a rabbit in a hole, and as Dave's father had taught him several times when he was young, you don't shoot prey you can't retrieve.

The retrieval of the body of Tammany Guileford would prove to be a monumental, distasteful chore, but Dave knew from experience that you can't claim to have taken a man's without a body to prove it.

The moon was briefly blacked out by passing clouds and when it shone again, Dave thought he saw his chance. In the changing light Guileford had managed to achieve a shelf along the side of the bluff. He was riding slowly now, looking up at the coulee, perhaps believing that he had achieved at least a part of his plan. Looking nearly straight down Dave could see that Guileford had accomplished nothing; there was no way up off the shelf.

Every movement of Guileford's now showed frustration clearly. He had made the wrong move, not a stupid move, but the wrong one. In Guileford's position, Dave thought that he himself would have likely done the same. With a hunter behind you, a fleeing man needs both distance and concealment. The coulee had seemed to offer both, but it had simply swallowed the outlaw up. Perhaps by daylight Guileford would have had a chance, but even the patchy moonlight was against him.

It was a good time for it, maybe the only chance at it. Dave decided — he was going down. Did he owe his badge that much? He was uncertain, but he owed it to the memory of Virgil Dodd and the unknown man who had died during the bank hold up at Medicine Bow, and those who would die in the future under the guns of Tammany Guileford — for there would be more. The killer was unlikely to suddenly sprout a conscience.

The piebald would stand, but he decided to hobble it anyway. Approaching the rim of the coulee he looked down to get his bearings again. He had brought a coil of rope from his saddle, but he saw no good anchor for it, and ended up tossing it aside. Both of his legs were fiery, unsteady, and shaky.

'You can do this,' he muttered to himself, feeling no certainty.

The plan, if it could be called such, was to move a little ahead of Guileford, lower himself into the coulee and conceal himself, awaiting Tammany's approach. It could be done — there was no problem with going down from here.

He was a little over a hundred feet above Tammany, who was taking his moment of frustration and turning it into a pause for rest. The rope would have helped, but having already jettisoned that idea, Dave stepped cautiously over the edge of the sandy bluff and began his descent through the shifting shadows of the night.

Dave was hoping Guileford would not look up and see him by some sudden shaft of clear moonlight. If he did he would have himself an unexpected moment of amusement.

Dave lost the purchase on his second step, and his legs were not quick enough or strong enough to break his tumble. A rock slipped from under the heel of one boot and his other found no support on the chalky bank. His ends reversed and he slid face-forward into the coulee, smothering curses. He kept his right hand clamped on the Colt into its holster, for to lose that was to lose the battle, and he was brought up sharply by a clump of greasewood where he lay silently, pistol in hand, praying he had not given up the game.

He heard nothing in the cold moonlit night, not the whicker of his own horse, for which he was grateful, not a night bird nor a slithering thing. There was no additional movement from Tammany Guileford, whom Dave thought now had paused fifty feet or so below him, fifty yards back.

Dave lay in silence, dust tickling at his nose, his Colt revolver in his right hand. He heard the creak of saddle leather then, and a low, grumbled curse. He shifted around with infinite patience trying to find a place he could peer through the thicket of greasewood and watch Guileford's approach.

The night remained quiet. There was a silence about it that has no word for it. The dust and disturbed leaves had fallen and settled, the insects made none of their small scuttling sounds. The wind had ceased its motion. Dave Chandler lay silently bleeding in his copse, motionless, his senses straining for any movement, any sound, any whisper of intent. The silence was so complete, the world so still, that at one point he began to wonder if he had died.

If he had, his resurrection was tumultuous, glaring and sudden.

'Rise up, lawman, or die where you are,' the familiar, scratchy voice of Tammany Guileford rang out. Dave rolled his head over to find that somehow Guileford had slipped down on him from the up-slope side. His body twitched almost involuntarily as he tried to shift himself to at least give himself a chance — there was no chance.

The dark figure stood over him, revolver in hand. Dave closed his eyes and prayed for the best. Gunfire erupted in the night. Dave heard a heavy dropping sound, a grunt, and after a few seconds pried his eyes open again . . . to see the sharp silhouette of Rodeo McCallum against the pale moon.

'Can you make it?' Rodeo asked in his laconic way.

'What . . . ?' Dave asked in a daze. 'How did you find us?'

'You two are playing in my backyard,' Rodeo answered. Dave Chandler learned later that the Duchess had directed Rodeo. How he had found them was of no importance at all.

He had, that was all. Dave Chandler, despite himself, was still among the living.

Temporarily at least. The bellow of another unseen man above them roared down the long, terrible canyon:

'Throw down your guns and hold your positions! This is Sheriff Bill Jackson out of Collier and I've got seven men with Winchesters watching you. Surrender or die!'

175

Dave, even feeling as he did, decided that he would rather live. He looked at Rodeo, who, still expressionless, uncurled his hand and let his Colt drop to the ground.

'Hold your fire, boys! This is Marshal David Chandler out of Cheyenne. What you heard was a Medicine Bow bank robber getting arrested!'

There was a minute or so of grumbling before Stout's voice boomed down the canyon again. 'All right, Chandler. I knew you were somewhere in the area. Come up and let's have a look at you. Who's that with you?'

'Why, it's the landowner Rodeo McCallum. Mind dropping a rope to pull us up, Sheriff?'

12

It went without saying that there would be a conference between the sheriff and all involved. They sat around the rough puncheon table Steamboat Bill had made for his wife in the early days. Sheriff Jackson was there, of course, although Rodeo McCallum had advised him to leave his posse outside to relax, water and tend to their ponies.

'To me,' Rodeo said in that calm, steely way of his, 'it's always seemed like a bad idea to get too many armed men in one place.'

'All right then,' Stout said hurriedly as if he were in a rush to finish this business and get back to the supper he had left on the stove. 'Chandler, it seems you know the most about this business. Why don't you run it past me one more time, so I'm clear on it.'

Dave started to do just that, but the

Duchess spoke up and no one was going to interrupt her. 'It began when I was foolish enough to think I could hire some men to help me drove my horses to market this year instead of accepting the McCallum boys offer as I usually do. I thought that they had done enough for me — and, after all, they had their own horses to see to . . . '

'Yes, ma'am,' a weary looking Sheriff Jackson said, in a tone which indicated he would appreciate having things speeded along. The Duchess's mouth tightened a little; she was aware of the sheriff's attitude. Probably she had planned in her mind how she would tell her story. But whereas she enjoyed a calm, casual conversation, the sheriff did not. He wanted to have business done and depart.

Becky spoke up. 'Well, how were we to know they were bank robbers or worse?'

Sheriff Jackson nodded and looked hopefully at Marshal Dave Chandler, who was used to concise reporting.

Without embellishment, Dave said, 'The Guileford gang had taken up residence on the Porter ranch. I became aware of this, and since I had warrants out of Medicine Bow with me for them, I decided to try to take them there.'

'Not by yourself, I take it,' Stout said, glancing at Rodeo. Rodeo said nothing, nor did Wynn McCallum, who had returned and now stood stolidly behind Becky Porter, who was pale and exhausted from the trials of the night.

'Of course not,' Dave said. 'Neighboring citizens were enlisted and together we managed to subdue the entire gang. The last of them — Tammany Guileford — you saw us run down back in the big coulee. I have their warrants right here . . . ' Dave said, fumbling with the wallet in the inside pocket of his leather vest. Sheriff Jackson held up a hand.

'That can all wait for another time, Marshal. I have no doubt that you did everything by the book.' He paused and cleared his throat more loudly than seemed necessary. 'That's not even what I came here to talk to you boys about. There's only two of you here,' he said looking directly at Rodeo, who was not a man you could intimidate with a hard look. Rodeo glanced at Wynn and nodded to the sheriff.

'That's what I count as well,' Rodeo finally replied.

'What's this about?' Dave asked a little testily. 'These boys have been with me for most of today, fighting the Guilefords.'

'Nothin',' Stout replied. 'It's just that we had a couple of men hold up the east-bound stage last night. 'Where were you this morning?' he asked Wynn, since he expected no answer from Rodeo.

'Standing watch up on the roof — that's where I was all night.'

'He was!' Becky blurted out. 'That's where he was when I fled our ranch.'

'All night?' Stout asked slyly.

'All night,' was Wynn's firm answer.

'And the kid?' Stout asked, meaning Kit McCallum.

'He's moved on,' Rodeo said. 'He don't live here any more.'

'That leaves Nick,' the sheriff persisted.

'Nick has moved on, too,' Rodeo said.

'Look here, Sheriff!' Dave Chandler said, now upset. 'Nick McCallum was with us at the raid on the Porter ranch. He was killed there — I witnessed it myself. A man can't be in two places at once! You've made some mistake in coming out here.'

'So it seems, Marshal,' Stout said, rising, adjusting his hat. 'When he's lost, a man will start following known trails. There was some confusion back there. One bold citizen was carrying his rifle in the coach with him. He swears he winged one of the hold-up men.' He looked from Wynn to Rodeo and back. 'It doesn't seem that either of you is carrying lead. If Nick, as you say, is dead . . . '

'It's not 'if we say',' Wynn said, now with a little heat. 'I brought him home

in a wagon. It wouldn't have been fittin'
to bury him with those Guileford skunks.
We'll make his grave on the Big M.'

Stout, standing now, nodded silently.
Wynn shouted out, 'Do you want to go
out to the stone corral with me? I can
show you his body!'

Sheriff Jackson looked only slightly
abashed. 'That leaves only Kit. Any idea
where he is?'

'You could start looking in Gato
Negro,' Becky said shakily. 'He hasn't
been here except to peek in.'

'Gato Negro! Why would he . . . ?'
Stout's comment fell to a mutter, seeing
the answer in Becky Porter's eyes. 'I'd
better go see if we can drag Tammany
Guileford's body up out of the ravine.
Bring the papers you're carrying into
Collier tomorrow, marshal. It'll give you
the chance to have the doctor look you
over, too.'

Near the door Sheriff Jackson paused.
The Duchess had scurried to catch up
with him.

'I'm sorry, Rose Ann,' he apologized

before she could say what was on her mind. 'You know I was just trying to do my job.'

'I know. Do you think any of your posse would like to take a job with me droving my herd to market?'

'I couldn't say — it could be, since their working for me seems to be over after tonight.'

'It would get them right back home where they started from,' Rose Ann said cheerfully. 'Do you mind if I put it to them? After all they've been through for me, I couldn't possibly ask the McCallums for help with that.'

'You can come out and ask my deputies, Duchess. A few of them might be pleased to have stumbled onto another job so soon.'

'I think I shall do that,' Rose Ann Porter said brightly. She took the arm he offered and they moved out into the moonlit yard. Stout's deputies roused themselves and moved forward for instructions.

Rose Ann said, 'I only need a few

good men. I hope there are two or three as honest and reliable as the McCallums. They're fine young men, Sheriff. Lord knows they saved the day for me. They're good neighbors, I can tell you. They are good boys, Mr Jackson, you can take my word for that.'

Sheriff Jackson nodded glumly, finding himself just a little ashamed of himself in the face of this woman's hard-won praise, and they walked on then against the moon-splotched yard.

We do hope that you have enjoyed reading this large print book.

Did you know that all of our titles are available for purchase?

We publish a wide range of high quality large print books including:
Romances, Mysteries, Classics
General Fiction
Non Fiction and Westerns

Special interest titles available in large print are:
The Little Oxford Dictionary
Music Book, Song Book
Hymn Book, Service Book

Also available from us courtesy of Oxford University Press:
Young Readers' Dictionary
(large print edition)
Young Readers' Thesaurus
(large print edition)

For further information or a free brochure, please contact us at:
Ulverscroft Large Print Books Ltd.,
The Green, Bradgate Road, Anstey,
Leicester, LE7 7FU, England.
Tel: (00 44) **0116 236 4325**
Fax: (00 44) **0116 234 0205**

QUARTER TO MIDNIGHT

Ned Oaks ·

Brutally attacked one night in the woods, Steve Karner hadn't been seen in years, and everyone in the Oregon town of Stayton thought him dead. Then the men who tried to kill him start dying, one by one; and it soon becomes apparent that Karner is not only alive, but riding a vengeance trail. But there are many dangers to be faced along the way, including a cunning young millionaire who will use all his family's power to protect his secrets, and a cold-blooded hired killer out for Karner's blood . . .